AF481179

The Adventures
of
Trading Post Kate

KEN KEITH

ISBN-9798702540306:

DEDICATION

This book is dedicated to my loving wife who has purchased and read romance novels since I can remember. She has spent a small fortune on paperback books and the few times I have read what she buys, I was confident that I could do better.

This book is also dedicated to all of you who have had sexual thoughts but were afraid to act on them, or even express them, because you thought you were the only one to have these thoughts. The fact is, that we all have some form of thoughts that fall outside of what our public persona says is socially acceptable. This book gives you an insight to what others have enjoyed for centuries

CONTENTS

1	CHAPTER ONE	1
2	CHAPTER TWO	7
3	CHAPTER THREE	11
4	CHAPTER FOUR	15
5	CHAPTER FIVE	21
6	CHAPTER SIX	29
7	CHAPTER SEVEN	36
8	CHAPTER EIGHT	39
9	CHAPTER NINE	45
10	CHAPTER TEN	49
11	CHAPTER ELEVEN	52
12	CHAPTER TWELVE	56
13	CHAPTER THIRTEEN	66
14	CHAPTER FOURTEEN	73
15	CHAPTER FIFTEEN	77
16	CHAPTER SIXTEEN	86
17	CHAPTER SEVENTEEN	93
18	CHAPTER EIGHTEEN	100
19	CHAPTER NINETEEN	109
20	CHAPTER TWENTY	117

PROLOGUE

We, as a people, seem to think that we have invented all things sexual and perverse in our lifetime. The truth is, that every emotion and perversion that exists today, existed hundreds, if not thousands of years ago and were practiced. Some sexual acts maybe more accepted today than they were a couple hundred years ago, but then other deviancies, that today would be punished by prison time, may have been common and were not punished at all. Just because everyone didn't have instant access to erotic material did not mean your ancestors did not have basal desires that they tried to satisfy.

Many people have a preconceived idea that the trail between St. Louis, Missouri and California was nearly devoid of civilized humans. As you will read, there were a great many people along the way. Many of them with the same desires you have today. While Kate is a fictional person, the story is as historically correct as I know, and depicts what her life may have been like.

1 CHAPTER ONE

The year was 1849 and the goldrush was just beginning. There were greatly exaggerated stories going around of the wealth to be had in the California Territory. St. Louis, Missouri was the primary staging ground for people, mostly men, going west over land. Some of the wealthy chartered a ship around the tip of South America but the cost was tremendous and most chose to travel by wagon. It was an exciting year for me because I was in my mid-teens and I had become aware of boys. I lived in St. Louis, Missouri with my Mother, Father, and two younger sisters.

My parents made me quit school after the eighth grade, saying that I needed to help mom and learn to run a household. I liked school and wished I could have gone longer. Moms housekeeping education for me could have been summarized in a single sentence. "Always do what your husband tells you to do, cook his meals and keep a clean home." I didn't need to stop school for that, I had seen it my whole life. Mother was always a fastidious cleaner, but recently a Cholera epidemic had broken out, in our town, and she felt cleaning would help keep it away, so she cleaned constantly.

My Father also benefited from my not going to school, as he had me help him in his hardware store down by the river. It was more than a hardware store, it could have been called a dry goods store as well, in that we sold everything but food. I was supposed to keep the books and ring up purchases but I often assisted customers, stocked shelves and even swept the floors. I was also designated to help ladies who wanted feminine things because my father felt they would be more comfortable asking a woman. Corsets were the rage, and most of the middle and upper crust ladies had one or more. The privileged purchased theirs from a clothier, but the more common lady would buy hers from my Father's store.

My Father also kept a selection of French postcards, for the men, in a cabinet just inside the store room door. If a customer asked, or they were regulars that he knew, he would let them go into the back room to look at the post cards and make their purchases. He always rang up those purchases, but I knew exactly what was in the cabinet because I often looked at the cards myself. They usually featured partially nude women, sometimes two or more women touching each other. They showed, clearly, their breasts but the area between their legs was usually a huge mass of black hair. They almost never showed a man's body but I found a couple that showed the man, apparently mating the woman, standing between her spread legs. One card, showed a man and a woman, doing it, while another man smoked his pipe and watched. For some reason, I was excited by those naughty pictures.

I liked working for my Father because of the men, especially the young men, who came in to buy things for their trip to the West. They paid me a lot of attention. Some paid so much attention that my Father would have to ask them to move along.

One such young man was Robert. He often came in and usually had a bit of saw dust on his clothes or in his beautiful brown hair. He was always looking for hinges and fasteners of various types. I think he worked for a cabinet shop or something but came to my Father's store near the end of the day to buy things for his own projects. I don't know if he really noticed me as he was always talking about how he wanted to go to California and how he had designed a wagon that was so much better than other wagons, for traveling.

My body was developing nicely, my breasts were already larger than many of the adult women I knew. I had a very nice flair to my hips, giving me the hour glass figure that men liked so much. Further, I had been having my monthly visitor, for the last three months like clockwork, so I felt I was already a woman. Being almost grown, I wanted to go out with my friends and be courted by a man, but my parents refused, saying I was too young.

I understood why my parents kept us from going out because the Cholera epidemic was running rampant and almost ten percent of the population, in St. Louis, had died from it. Many blamed the large influx of people coming into town on steamers and other means, for the illness. As I said, I understood why I was not allowed to go out, but I wanted desperately to go to dances and socials to be courted by a man. Here I was 17, almost 18 and I had never even been kissed.

After much begging and complaining, my dad finally agreed to let me go to the church social, after church, on Sunday. There would be ice cream and most likely music and dancing of some kind. But the most important thing to me was the fact that there would be young men there, who just might ask me for a dance or ask to escort me home.

The social was very exciting, there must have been fifty people there and many of them I had not seen before. I stood with my friend, Emily, and we giggled as we chatted about the different guys we would like to dance with. Emily was pointing out the ones who she thought would be good lovers. Emily was like that.

Emily was my age and lived, with her mother, in a small flat near my Father's hardware store. She used to live near us, on the Bluffs overlooking the Mississippi River, but when her father suddenly died from the Cholera, they were forced to sell their home and move to a small flat. We didn't know how they made ends meet and the church was unable to provide much assistance because so many had succumbed to the disease, leaving many families without support and needing help. We heard rumors that Emily's mother had a few gentleman callers, who would stay for an hour or so and then leave. Many widows were forced to do this, to make ends meet, and even though it was frowned upon, no one said much because it was needed for survival. Emily told me that her mom would take her friends into her bedroom to "talk" and lock the door. Emily claimed she could hear them moaning passionately and the bed squeaking behind the door.

Both Emily and I were at the age where sexual things were of interest to us, but neither of us had the resources to learn much. I got ideas from the postcards I looked at, and she got her ideas from what she imagined, and overheard, her mother doing.

We each danced with a couple boys that attended our church but they were younger than we were so it was awkward and not much fun. Later, when it was almost dark, a handsome man, I had not seen earlier, asked me to dance. It was Robert, the young man who often visited my Father's hardware store. I almost did not recognize him, all dressed up. I accepted his request to dance, but I was so flustered that I am sure he thought I had never danced before. He would have been correct, in that I had never danced with a stranger before. My sisters and I had practiced dancing, for many hours, with the Victrola Phonograph and on special occasions I would dance with my Father. We danced three dances in a row and I felt that this was the most exciting thing that had ever happened to me. I also noticed that I became very damp between my legs. Emily said it was a sure sign that I was in love, but I just hoped he would ask my Father if he could call on me for a date.

Robert waited till Saturday afternoon, just as we were closing for the day, to come into the hardware store. He purchased a can of paint, some turpentine and a couple paint brushes. I made sure to ring up his purchases and while he paid me, he asked if I would like to go get some ice cream that evening. I hadn't had a chance to prepare for the date, so I told him he had to ask my Father and that even if my Father said it was okay, it would have to be after seven in the evening. Robert asked my Father who thought about his request for a minute and then said he would allow it, but that I had to be home before dark. It was summer and dark was about 9:30 so I had inadvertently limited my date to just a couple hours. I was excited just the same.

The minute Robert left, I begged my father to let me go home early so I could bathe and prepare for my first date. He teased me, saying that since the young man had asked me for a date, I was apparently good enough in my work clothes, but then grinned and told me to run along.

I did all the things a woman does to make herself ready and put on one of my nicest summer dresses. I bathe and even used a drop of Mother's perfume. You can imagine my disappointment, when Robert turned up fifteen minutes late, still wearing what he had on earlier. It looked like he had made an effort to dust himself off but he had paint smudges on his hands and clothes. He smelled like linseed oil and turpentine.

We walked to the ice cream shop, as it was only a few blocks past my Father's store and the store was less than a quarter mile from our house. Robert explained that he had wanted to get his first coat of paint on his wagon and it had taken longer than he had expected. I sort of forgave him and we each enjoyed a bowl of ice cream.

Robert talked incessantly about his wagon and his plans to go to California. His enthusiasm was infectious and I told him that I wanted to see his wagon sometime as he walked me home. It was shortly after that that he caught my hand and held my hand as we walked to my home. He didn't kiss me at the gate, and I don't know what I would have done if he did, but I was the happiest girl in St. Louis because he had held my hand for the last several blocks.

Robert began visiting the hardware store almost every day, He usually bought something, even if it was a few nails or screws but I made sure to wait on him each time. When he asked me out, for the coming Saturday afternoon, I quickly answered yes. He told me that he would bring the wagon he had built and take me for a drive. This time I was unsure how to dress, since the last time he had arrived smelling of paint, so I just wore a nice dress that had a high waist, giving me some support and accentuating my breasts. Since we planned to ride, and because I wanted him to see how mature I was, I chose not to bind my breasts.

2 CHAPTER TWO

Saturday soon arrived and my father allowed me the day off from work, with instructions that I be home before nightfall. Robert showed up, shortly after noon, driving a huge green and white painted wagon, pulled by a pair of the largest Percheron Horses I had ever seen. They must have been 19 or 20 hands tall and pulled the heavy wagon like it was nothing. Robert claimed his Poppa had won them in a card game. This time, Robert had his good clothes on and I was somewhat embarrassed that I had decided to wear one of my plainer dresses.

We rode down along the river road, past the ferries and along the tree lined road until Robert found a spot that made a natural beach. He parked the wagon and helped me down. We walked along the shore with him holding my hand as he shared his dreams of adventure in the gold fields. When we returned to the wagon, he showed me the many unusual features he had designed into it. The best one, I thought, was that the seat had springs and a padded seat. It was a very comfortable ride even on a rough road. The sides were tall and had large shelves that he explained could be lowered and used as shelves or as a bed. There was barely room for both of us to stand between the lowered shelves and it was there, he kissed me. I thought he was going to move past me but he gently pushed me back against the shelf and kissed me. It was a terribly forward move to kiss me but I allowed it and even kissed him back as no one could possibly see what we were doing in the enclosed wagon.

I was feeling things I had never felt before. My heart was beating so hard I thought he must have surely been able to hear it and my breathing sounded like I had run all the way home from my Father's hardware store. I knew it was wrong, but I really didn't want to stop him from kissing me. Under my clothes my nipples were as hard as they had ever been and they tingled more than they ever did when I touched myself. If Emily was correct, about it being a sure sign that you were in love if you got damp between your legs, then I must have been head over heels in love because I could tell I was absolutely wet down there. I had a burning itch, that begged to be scratched.

Robert hands were caressing my back, sometimes getting close to my bottom, but always moving back up to my shoulders. He suddenly moved one hand to my breast and cupped it while pinching the nipple between his fingers. I don't know what I would have done, if he had caressed it gently, but he was excited too and when he pinched my tender nipple, it hurt and I yelped, pushing him away. Robert was a good kisser, and I wondered if he had kissed other girls, but his attempts to touch my body were clumsy. He tried to go back to kissing me, but I told him that I wanted him to take me home, since he couldn't behave himself and chose to take liberties. Deep down, I was excited beyond belief, but I had allowed him to go much further than I should have, this early in our relationship. Emily always said that after you were engaged you could pet but if you allowed a suitor to touch you before that, he would consider you easy.

At first, Robert apologized but when I stood my ground, he became angry and didn't speak as he took me home with the horses at a trot. When we arrived at my house he just said, "Your home", without looking at me. I felt bad, for ruining our date, and told him that I had to stop him as it was not proper unless we were engaged to be married. Robert grinned and gave me a chaste kiss, on my cheek, before I climbed down from the wagon.

That night, I lay in bed and relived the sensations I had felt during our date earlier. It was very warm out, so I slipped my night gown off and lay naked under the sheets. My hands rubbed my tender breasts as well as up and down my body to the patch of hair between my legs. Just thinking about it made me damp down there and caused my nipples to throb. This caused a wonderful feeling to form between my legs. It was like I could fan a tiny coal into full flame just by thinking about what I had done. I silently wished I had not pushed Robert away when he pinched my nipple. I tormented my breasts by pinching my nipples, hard, while I thought about what I had allowed Robert to do. I lay there with my legs opened wide gently bucking against an invisible paramour. I silently wondered what would have happened if I had not pushed Robert away. That night, when I touched myself, it made my whole-body tremble.

The next week, Robert did not come to the store until Wednesday. I was worried that, my attempt to be a good girl, had caused him not to be interested in me anymore. When he finally came into the store, he had a man with him that made me a bit nervous. Robert introduced the man as his Poppa, and asked to see my Father in private. The three of them went into his private office. My Father's office had large windows that faced into the store and I could see that initially everyone was all smiles but the more they talked the more heated their discussion became. Because I was the only person in the store to help customers, I could not watch everything but at one point I heard my Father yell, "There will be no G** D*m*d dowry! and if you don't like it that's too bad because she is too young to get married anyway!" Until that point, I had assumed they were discussing business or maybe asking for a line of credit. What I, and everyone in the store at that time, heard could only mean Robert had asked for my hand in marriage. I was so distracted that I accidentally gave a customer change for twenty dollars when he had just given me a dollar. Fortunately, he was honest and informed me of my mistake. He smiled as he gave me back the extra money. Now I was embarrassed and distracted.

Shortly after my father's outburst, the two men left. At my first chance I asked my father what they had wanted. He looked at me, with a certain sadness, and told me he would explain it all to me after the store had closed. Someone, on the city council, had decided that it would be good business if all the stores stayed open late one night each week and tonight was the night. It was only two more hours until we closed the store but they were the longest two hours of my young life.

With agonizing slowness, the clock finally reached closing time and I quickly locked the front door as the last customer left. I hurried back to my Father who did not seem to be anxious to talk to me. He suggested that we sit in his office where he produced a bottle of whiskey from one of his desk drawers. He poured a generous portion into an enameled metal cup and then added a couple inches of water to mine, almost filling the cup. He handed me my cup and told me to drink up, that I would need it. He was beginning to worry me because, beyond a sip of wine once in a while, I had never tasted alcohol. Now he was giving me as much as he was drinking. He told me he added the water to make it easier for me to drink but it still burned like fire as I sipped the amber liquid

3 CHAPTER THREE

.

We sat in silence drinking for a few minutes while my Father gathered his thoughts and I fretted over what I was about to hear. The whiskey was going down easier with each sip. Finally, my father spoke. "Katie, you've grown into a beautiful woman. Every man that comes into this store cannot help but stare at your breasts." He stopped for a second and looked right at my breasts before continuing. "You are more attractive than your mother was when she was young."

I didn't know my father had even noticed my breasts and I beamed as he compared me favorably against my mother. It felt kind of heady to be sitting in front of my Father as he talked about my breasts. I don't know if it was the booze or some other reason but I was not ashamed and may have even sat up a little straighter to push my titties forward.

He continued, "Today, that nice young man came to me and asked for your hand in marriage." I took a large swallow of my drink and don't remember it burning at all. "And Katie, baby, I told him Yes. You are a bit young but I have known other couples that have made it. Besides, I am afraid that the Cholera is going to kill us all, so maybe going to California will be a good thing". I jumped up and hugged my Father and was crying as I told him that I loved him. We hugged for a long time before my Father refilled my now empty cup, this time with a bit less water, and told me that I may not be quite so happy when I hear the rest of the facts.

I sat and again sipped the strong drink. It was making me feel a bit woozy. He continued that Robert was very respectful but that his Father or Poppa as he referred to him, had demanded a dowry. My father said he acted like his son would be doing us a large favor by marrying me and that they should be compensated for it. I was instantly so angry that I was crying, this time from anger. How dare they think my Father should pay to have me married off. I no longer cared if Robert ever called again!

My father told me that they had walked out saying that it was their way or no way. I was again hugging my Father and this time crying and telling him that it was okay and I never wanted to see Robert again. In those few minutes I had learned that my Father saw me as a woman, that my boyfriend wanted to marry me and that I wasn't going to get married and I didn't really care. I finished the second cupful.

I was going on about how I didn't care when my Father stopped me and told me that Robert's father was a professional gambler and somewhat of a con man. He said that he thought that he may have been bluffing, after all, he had played some poker too. Something else I hadn't known about my Father. He said that if Robert had real feelings for me, he would be back with his hat in his hand. I wasn't very confident that he would come back but held my cup out for another shot. This time he poured two fingers directly into the cup and handed it back to me.

Everything was fine until I tried to get up to walk home with my Father. Suddenly the room was spinning and my Father had to help me walk. He let me sit for a few minutes while he ran next door to borrow a buggy from a friend of his. My Father's best friend ran a store right next to my Father's store and they often shared things. He helped me into the buggy and sat next to me with his arm around me to support me. It was already dark, so we had been talking for a lot longer than I remembered, as we rode home with me snuggled against my Father. I don't know if was accidental or if he too was feeling the effects of the whiskey, but his hand cupped my breast from the side for a little while. Maybe he was just confirming that I had grown up.

We arrived home to a very angry Mother. She was ranting about us being late and almost screaming that she couldn't believe he had gotten me drunk. She carried on for a while until father told her, "She received some very bad news today so just be quiet", ...and she did. I could tell she was upset but she set out our dinner for us and was polite.

Maybe drinking whiskey, for the first time, on an empty stomach was not a very good idea but I felt a bit better after eating a little and went to my room to sleep it off.

My eighteenth birthday came and went and although this made me legally old enough to marry without parental permission, I was not in the mood to marry anyone after what had happened with Robert.

Robert did not return to the store for a week. I was sad, but was trying to put it behind me. The next week, I had just started having my monthly visitor and this time it had returned with a vengeance.

I was cramping and felt awful but I tried to keep working in the store. Just before lunch my Father put a kettle of water on to heat and then went to a shelf and took down a ceramic flask that held about a quart but was flattened on one side. He poured the hot water in the bottle, capped it with a cork and told me to go lay down in the storage room and to put the bottle where it hurts. Once again, I could not believe how perceptive my Father was and how he knew about my female problems. The warm flask felt heavenly and while I still had cramps, I was able to continue working.

Robert chose this day, just before closing, to come see me and ask for a date. I lit into him asking what was wrong with him and asked him, with as much venom as I could muster, if he had decided that I could be had without a dowry. He apologized, saying that the dowry was his Poppa's idea and that he didn't even know that his Poppa intended to ask my Father for one, until they were in the office. He told me he was angry with his Poppa but had been ordered not to return for a week. After a week had passed, his Poppa decided that we were not going to pay a dowry and told his son that he could again court me if he wanted to. I kind of accepted his story but told him to call me next week and I would give him my answer.

The minute he left I felt on top of the world again and the cramps didn't seem as bad. I knew I would forgive him and my Father just grinned at me all the time. I had told Robert to call next week knowing that, by then, my visitor would be gone, but he didn't wait that long. Three days later, he showed up at my house, after work, all dressed up and with his hat in his hand, just like Father had said. I met him in the parlor and he got down on one knee and asked me to marry him. Of course, I said yes and cried as he put a simple golden band on my finger. I say golden rather than gold because it turned my finger green, but it was beautiful to me. When I looked at my Father, he had tears in his eyes too and told me to "Not be too late" before I even asked the question.

4 CHAPTER FOUR

I had relived what Robert and I had done on our last date so many times and I had decided, even before he had proposed, that if he tried to touch my breasts again, I was going to let him touch as much as he wanted to. He kissed me in front of my parents and then escorted me out to his wagon. We rode around town, had ice cream and, again, ended up down near the river. This time when he stopped, we did not go for a walk and I practically drug him into the back. We kissed and it felt so good. Robert was being very circumspect with his hands. He rubbed my back some but was not going to risk a fight if he touched my breast.

We were again standing in the narrow center walkway and when we took a break from kissing, I took his rough workman's hand and placed it on my breast. I whispered "They are yours now...just be gentle" Robert was a fast learner and in no time, he was expertly cupping both of my breasts. I turned with my back towards him and he reached around my body to fondle my breasts while kissing my neck. I was in heaven.

I could feel his hardness poking into my lower back and reached behind myself to feel him through his trousers. I had never felt a man before but it seemed awfully big and very hard. I knew the basic theory of sex but I was not sure something that big would go inside me. Robert wanted me to take it out but I told him that would not happen until our wedding night. I unbuttoned the top of my dress and he soon had his hands on my bare breasts. Sometimes in his excitement he would pinch my nipples a little too hard but I loved what he was doing. He kept rubbing his hardness against my bottom until he kind of jerked. Robert turned red and told me that he needed to go home because he had made a mess in his pants. Since I knew nothing about what happened to a man, actually I knew almost nothing about what happened to a woman, so I though he had peed himself and laughed at him telling him he was now my "Baby". What was meant to be a teasing remark, became his nickname from me, even after I learned what happens when a man gets too excited. We straightened ourselves out and returned home. This time he walked me to the door and kissed me before I went inside.

We dated twice each week and went to church together on Sunday. Almost every time we would find ourselves down by the river. The day I let Robert, my Baby, suck on my breasts I almost let him have his way with me. He had been asking if he could touch me, down there, and I wanted to know how good it might feel. He suckled me like a little baby, as I reached under my dress to removed my petticoat and drawers. Even though all of my drawers were crotchless and did not cover my womanhood, I removed them so I could let Robert touch my bottom. I am sure he saw most of my legs and part of my bottom as I removed my undergarments but that is what I had planned. The act of letting my future husband see my private parts was very exciting to me. It was exciting for Robert too. Tonight, the lump in his pants seemed even larger than usual.

I unbuttoned the front of my dress and pulled my breasts completely out for him to see. It was exciting to let him see my bare breasts and I was anxious to know what his hands would feel like on my bare bottom. He stopped sucking my nipples and just looked at me. I felt a tingle all the way to my toes as I stood before him and let him push my dress the rest of the way off. Robert drew me closer and ran his hands over of my legs and all across my bottom. Because we were in his wagon, we were standing so close that we were almost touching. I am sure he saw my front but I would not let him look, between my legs, I did not stop him when he touched me there. His touch felt heavenly. When he felt how wet I had become, he asked if I had peed myself. I don't know if he was getting back at me for my comment a couple weeks earlier or if he didn't know anything about a woman's body. Either way it broke the moment and I didn't let him go any further than sucking my titties and feeling me down there.

Robert wanted a quick wedding so we could be on our way to California. I wanted a quick wedding so we could be together every night. Because of this and because everyone was afraid that the Cholera would soon kill everyone, sour wedding was planned quickly. There was a flurry of activity trying to get ready for a wedding in just one month's time. I am sure our friends thought that I was with child, which is why most people usually got married quickly. Our reasons were different, and neither one of us really cared what other people thought. Robert wanted to go to California as part of the gold rush. Like everyone else he hoped to become rich collecting the gold that was supposedly just lying there to be claimed. Robert also knew that people would pay dearly for the comforts they gave up on the East coast as well as for the things they needed to mine gold and survive.

One of the things my parents did during the month before our wedding, was to invite Robert's Poppa, William, to dinner to build the relationship between our families. As I got to know William, he was no longer scary to me. In fact, I loved to listen to his stories. Like his son, his excitement was contagious. I was always left wondering if his stories were true, but they were fun to hear. I also learned that William would be traveling to California with us. I was disappointed to be told this because I had imagined Robert and I making love in the wagon every night. That would be impossible, with a third person in the wagon. I was also concerned that Robert's poppa kept saying that I would be a big asset to them on the trail and once we reached California. I was not marrying William, I was marrying his son; I was not a horse or a piece of land that had value as an asset.

During that month I also met Nate, a friend of Roberts. Robert had chosen Nate to be his best man. Robert and I conspired to have a double date with Emily, my maid of honor, but we ran out of time too soon. Nate was a small guy but he was very strong. He earned his living shoeing horses for many people around town. I liked Nate because he was Robert's best friend and because he was always cracking jokes. He could also draw beautifully.

My Mother let me use a cream colored dress that she had bought mail order. She had planned to wear it to church and on special occasions, but thought it would be a beautiful dress for me to be married in. I thought it was beautiful and knew the dress would serve me well, in my new life. It was not bulky with tons of extra material like some wedding dresses and like most wedding dresses, it could be used for many years for church or other dress up occasions.

 Our church agreed to let us have our wedding before services on Sunday with the understanding that if anyone had succumbed to the Cholera, we would allow the funeral to go first.

I think that Robert and his Poppa had hoped that I would have a dowry to fund their trip to California but my parents, while comfortable, were not rich. Since my Father was in the hardware business Robert requested two things from my father. A top of the line wood stove that had a reservoir to hold warm water and a fancy bathing tub. My parents gave us those as part of our wedding presents along with several bolts of cloth and misc. hardware items.

My Mother had not told me what to expect on my wedding night and with the wedding tomorrow, at noon, I wanted to know. I asked her while she was letting out the bosom of what would be my wedding dress to accommodate my larger breasts. Since she did not talk about things like this, her answer was predictably short. "After the wedding is over and you get to the hotel, he will want to do IT, so you go in the bathroom, if there is one in the room, or at least behind the privacy screen and put your nightgown on. Then you turn out the gaslight and get in bed with him. He will know what to do, you just let him do what he wants. You should never tell him "No". She mumbled something about "It hurts like hell the first few times but it gets better after that." I attempted to ask her what I did once I was in his bed but she refused to explain, saying "He will tell you what to do."

I was not sure why I was supposed hide to get changed for bed since I was going to be married to this man and he would probably see me change every night from now on. I also assumed that she had no idea that I had already let him see most of my body. I was no closer to knowing what to do than I was before I asked my Mother and I was pretty sure Robert didn't have a clue. When my Aunt and Uncle came to our house, after the wedding rehearsal at the church, I asked my aunt to come to my room. My aunt Rose had always been quite forward so I asked her what I should expect. Her answer was much more graphic and included explanations of exactly where he was going to put his fingers and penis. The really scary part was how big she said a man's penis was when he was hard and ready to mate. As for the hurting, she predicted that since Robert was ten years older than me, he would have some experience and be gentle. She told me that my first time may hurt, but it would not be as bad as I had imagined. She gave me the only practical advice I had received for my wedding night. Aunt Rose suggested that I take a small jar from the pantry and fill it with lard. She suggested that when I put my night gown on, I should rub a generous amount, on my lady parts, to make it easier for my new husband to enter my body.

As we went to join the family in the sitting room she whispered in my ear, "You know you should leave your underwear off under your night gown, right?" I giggled and said I knew but until that moment I was planning on leaving my underwear and a camisole on because the night gown Emily had given me, for my first night, was very sheer.

My friend Emily and I had talked about our wedding night frequently, when we were alone together, but it was in romantic girlish terms of how our future husband would carry us to our marital bed and make gentle love to us for hours. As I would learn later, I was going into my marriage with only a vague idea of what would happen.

The big day came and I had packed a small carpet bag with the clothes I would wear the first night and an outfit for the following day. Emily was may maid of honor and was as excited as I was about my wedding. We got to the church early and prepared for the ceremony. Since it was fall there were not a lot of flowers for my hair and my bouquet, but someone found a few sunflowers and a smaller flower that looked a lot like the sunflowers that we could weave into my hair.

It seemed like only minutes later the piano began to play the wedding march and my Father was waiting for me to escort me down the aisle. I felt beautiful as I slowly walked toward Robert, Nate, and the preacher. Nate seemed proud that Robert had chosen him to be his best man and witness.

The ceremony was brief and even though I worried that I would forget when to say "I do" we both got through it. Robert kissed me in front of the whole church and it was a long kiss. Since our wedding was held before church services, we then had to sit through a two-hour sermon in our heavy dress clothes before we could have our reception in the basement of the church. The reception had so much food, an army could not have eaten it all. There was dancing where I danced with my father and my new husband before everyone else had a turn with me. I must have danced thirty dances straight. I was exhausted and my feet hurt before we left.

5 CHAPTER FIVE

Robert, of course was in a hurry to leave so we could start our honeymoon. Our honeymoon was a night, in the honeymoon suite, of a downtown hotel arraigned for us by William. Even though I was tired, I was giddy because I was now Mrs. Robert Cave. I was also nervous about what was going to happen when we got there.

Even signing in was embarrassing. The desk clerk had a big booming voice and referred to me as the blushing bride. I am sure I was blushing, because I was sure everyone in the lobby knew we were going to go up the steps to our room and have sex for the first time. The good part, of signing in, was I got to write my married name for the first time, Mrs. Robert Cave.

The bellhop escorted us to our room and then left. Robert and I looked at each other and he pulled me close and kissed me. We stood there kissing but it was still hot in the room and I had been in my hot wedding dress of almost nine hours. I wanted to get out of my dress but I was terrified of what was going to happen the minute I did.

When I couldn't take it anymore, I suggested that Robert help me out of my dress and I reminded him that I promised him that on our wedding day he would see all of me and I would touch his manhood as well. Robert wasted no time in helping me undo the dozen little buttons and hooks that held the dress together. As it slipped from my shoulders and my breasts came into view, I held my dress over them and retreated behind the privacy screen in the room.

In my haste, I forgot my carpet bag and had to ask Robert to please hand it to me over the screen. Most screens were low and the person changing could easily see over the top. The one in our room was very tall, probably to give nervous brides a moment of privacy before the big event. I told my new husband to get ready to make me his wife as I removed the dress and petticoats and stood behind the screen letting the breeze from the open windows cool my skin. I took my aunts advice and removed every stitch of clothing and then and put on the sheer nighty. I may just as well had left it off as it hid nothing. It barely covered my breasts, leaving my tummy bare and had a pair of drawers or panties that were closed in the crotch and not crotchless like my everyday drawers. I giggled as I considered that you would have thought that tonight, of all nights in my life, the drawers should have been open for easy access. The material was so sheer that you could see the dark hair under the panties and the color of the area around my nipples also showed through.

I remembered, at the last minute about, the lard and forced a large dollop inside myself with my finger. I asked Robert if he was ready for his bride and then asked him to shut out the lights. Robert said he was ready, but he wanted the lights on until he saw his beautiful bride. I remembered that I should always defer to him so I plucked up my courage, after all he had seen my breasts many times and I am sure he had seen most of me, especially my legs and my bottom when I let him remove my dress, in his wagon so I guess he could see all of me now. Besides, he said I was beautiful and I kind of liked the idea of being naked in front of my new husband.

I held my chin up and walked out from behind the screen to stand near the foot of the bed we would soon share. I had expected Robert to be under the covers but he was totally nude and laying on his back on top of the covers. His manhood looked absolutely huge. I had never seen an erect male and I stared at what had to be 6 or 7 inches long and fat with a pointed end. There is no way something that big could fit inside me. I began to wonder if maybe he just put the pointed tip in and his seed was injected into my lady parts. I also remembered my Mother saying it hurt like Hell, the first few times and then got better.

I stood basically nude letting my husband see what he had married. He sat up to have a better look. While I was proud of my breasts, because I knew they were bigger and fuller than many other women, I was shy about him looking at my womanhood. He made a motion with his finger indicating that I should turn around. So, I turned around and let him see my backside. The tiny drawers I was wearing covered me a little but I still felt he could see everything. When I turned back around my husband said he wanted to see my tits, not breasts or boobs. He called them tits tonight. I pulled the filmy top off and let it drop onto the floor.

My new husband then wanted to see "The rest of it" so I pushed the panties down and stepped out of them. I had worn my nighty for less than one minute before removing it. I stood naked as the day I was born for his approval. He again made the motion with his finger indicating I should turn around. This time he saw my bare bottom, only a few feet away. When I turned back to face him, he crooked his finger so that I would come closer to the side of the bed. I was shaking with excitement as I took the few steps to where he sat. The bed was quite low and when I stood in front of him, his face was almost level with my woman parts. With a deliberate slowness he reached up and ran his fingertips through the hair between my legs and rubbed me there. This caused my knees to buckle and me to moan loudly. He moaned too and without touching himself his semen shot from his penis and landed on his chest and legs. I had a brief thought that maybe I would not have to endure him putting it inside me tonight, since he had already shot his sperm. I hurried to the wash basin for a wash cloth and returned to carefully wipe the sticky goo from his body.

I decided that this would be a good time to fulfill my promise and as I knelt beside the bed, I held his penis and gently stroked him with one hand while I felt his balls move in his scrotum with my other hand. A man felt so much different than when I touched myself. I was amazed at how it felt as well as how thick it was. I could not close my hand around it. I wanted to make love even though I was still seriously concerned about his huge thing going inside my body. I climbed onto the bed with him and we began to kiss.

When we kissed in the wagon, I always made sure that we remained standing, even though Robert wanted us to lay in the bunks he had built. I refuse to let us go there because I knew I might not resist his advances. Our time in his wagon was usually after dark and hurried as I needed to get home soon so our explorations consisted of urgent groping while we kissed for a few minutes. Tonight, we had all the time in the world and we explored each other slowly, but urgently, with all the lights still left on.

We kissed passionately as I lay on top of my man and rubbed my body against his. The feeling of my nipples dragging through the course hair on his chest was exquisite. Robert turned me over while he carefully examined my breasts, in the light, while he suckled them and his hand moved down my body to the prize between my legs.

We returned to kissing but his fingers continued to explore my nether regions. He seemed unsure about putting his finger inside me. My Aunt had told me that my husband would push his finger all the way into my body like a miniature version of his penis. I could put my finger quite deep before it felt uncomfortable so I opened my legs wider and pushed my pelvis against his hand. It felt so wanton to do this with my new husband.

I had never masturbated with anything other than my finger tips and my imagination. Even though I was not a frail girl, my fingers were much smaller than Roberts. The feeling was exquisite as he probed deeper but he soon reached a point where it caused me a bit of pain. I thought that if his finger hurt there was no way I could stand to have his whole penis inside me. I again thought that I hoped he would only put it in just a little to make a seal as he squirted his sperms into me.

I tried to tough it out but as he pushed deeper it caused me to wince and he withdrew. I told him that it was OK but he asked if he could look at me down there. Of course, tonight of all nights I told him that I was his to use as he wanted. Inside I was totally embarrassed as I lay before him with my legs apart. He moved down the bed and used his fingers to gently open my folds and looked right up into me.   I was holding my breath when I felt a trickle of my moisture trickle out and down my fanny. As he studied my woman parts I noticed that he was getting hard again.

I told him that he had the rest of our lives to study me but that right now I wanted another kiss. He moved over me and I felt his erection brush the inside of my thigh. I quickly scooted out from under him and became the one on top. I kissed him and then straddled him and let the length of his penis slide along my furrow. Instinctively, I sat on him and worked my hips to masturbate my lover. My excess moisture caused it to slide easy and felt extremely good to me and soon both Robert and I were panting. I was focused on the good feelings I was receiving and didn't notice that Robert was nearly ready to come again.

His cock, as he called it, had become as large as ever and he pushed me off at the last second. He was almost rough as he forced me off and then apologized, saying he had to stop me or he would have climaxed again and may not have been able to complete our marriage tonight. Now I did not think that was such a bad idea but deep down I too wanted to officially become a woman tonight. I told my husband that I understood and wanted him to take my virginity tonight.

I began kissing my way down his chest remembering a conversation I had with Emily where she told me that she had learned somewhere, probably from her Mother, that men absolutely love it if you take their penis into your mouth and suck gently. I wasn't sure I wanted to put the thing he pees with, in my mouth but at the last moment I had an idea and began to rub my breasts on his penis. When I rubbed the tip of his penis across my nipples, he came, shooting a huge load of sperm across my breasts and some even landed on my chin. This time it was Robert who jumped up to rinse out the wash cloth and wipe the white stuff off of me while he apologized profusely.

If I had accepted his apology, he may not have been able to get erect again but after he wiped my chin, I kissed him hard and told him that for the rest of his life he could shoot his sperm anywhere he wants. This excited him so much that his cock never became soft. Soon Robert had me on my back and he was between my legs.

It was about to happen. My husband was poking around but missing the mark. I had my legs open but flat on the bed, when I remembered that in one of the post cards that I had seen, the woman had her legs wide apart and her knees bent. I took a deep breath before I let my legs open wider and bent my knees like I remembered the woman did on the post card. His penis found its mark and he had the tip of his penis firmly in my opening. I was frightened and asked him not to go too deep.

He held his position and kissed me. Then, while looking into my eyes, he said it is best to just get my virginity broken quickly. The clock in the hall had just began to chime midnight when he pushed hard. I felt a fullness followed shortly by a sharp pain. I cried out and he stopped pressing for just a second, while he covered my mouth with his, and pushed again until he was completely inside me. It burned like fire and I wanted him not to move so I wrapped my legs around him to hold him still. That really didn't work, but it did help align my love tunnel and he relaxed long enough to kiss me again.

He whispered after a bit that I was now a woman and even though it still was burning, I was crying from happiness, not pain. I told him that I wasn't truly a woman till he had shot off in me and he began to move. My first plan, of hoping he would cum and not be up to deflowering me tonight, came back to haunt me. Even though Robert was careful as he stroked himself in and out of my vagina, he continued inside me until the clock in the hall was striking the quarter hour. Fifteen minutes for your first time is forever and I was relieved when he began to pump faster and then held himself deep inside and came for a third time that night.

He climbed off of me and put his arm around me but was asleep instantly. I was exhausted too but got up to see how much damage he had done to my vagina. There was a bit of blood on me and on the sheets but not at all like I had heard it would be. I expected to see what looked like someone or something had been slaughtered, but there were only couple of, silver dollar sized, stains on the bedding and when I wiped myself, I could tell there was blood and more of the white stuff from him. I cleaned myself as much as I could before slipping back into bed, next to him, I chose to remain nude.

Again, that may not have been a good idea because when Robert woke up in the middle of the night, and found me nude next to him, he began to climb aboard once again. I tried to accommodate him, after all my Mother said I should always do what he wanted, but my vagina burned like fire. I winced when he touched me and had to stop him before he entered me again. Earlier, I had been excited and the pain did not seem too bad, but my torn hymen as well as the stretching and irritation from him being inside me for so long, made me so tender that I could not let him penetrate me again.

I stopped him and asked him not to do it now because I was sore. He bluntly told me that I was now his wife and I should not refuse him his conjugal rights. I pleaded with him and explained how sore my first time had made me. I offered to use my hand to pleasure him and he refused, but when I offered to let him rub it on my breasts again, he agreed after he extracted a promise from me, on our marriage, that after I was no longer sore I would, one night, do whatever he wanted sexually no matter what it was. That thought was a bit scary but it was a fun scary. I thought he may want me to put it in my mouth or again shoot his seed on my breasts but I was willing to do that to be spared the pain tonight.

This time Robert got a damp washrag and when he came back to our bed, he climbed over me and straddled my chest so that his penis lay in the valley between my breasts. He began moving it over my breasts and soon asked me to push my tits together. When I did, it formed a warm tunnel for his pleasure and he pumped his penis into it like it was my vagina. On the in stroke he was almost touching my lips. When he climaxed, he pulled back but his sperm went all over my face and breasts. He quickly said he was sorry and began wiping me clean but I could tell he had really enjoyed himself and was glad we found another way to have sex.

6 CHAPTER SIX

The next morning, which was only about three hours later at this point, he tried again, assuming I would no longer be sore. However, he didn't object when I reached between us and stroked his cock until he came in my hand. We checked out of the hotel and it seemed like the desk clerk was looking at me differently like he knew what we did in bed last night. We hadn't done anything wrong as far as I was concerned so I held my head high. I am sure I was blushing but I tried not to show it.

We went for breakfast in a cafe down the street and then after retrieving our wagon and horses from the livery stable we rode back to my home to retrieve all my worldly possessions which amounted to a couple boxes. The stove and washtub that my parents had given us were also loaded at the store and after hugs from everyone we rode down to the river landing to begin our life together. We went to an open field, where people gathered as they prepared to build a wagon train and head west. This time of the year there were only a few wagons there and we found a place to camp a little further back from the others to insure our privacy.

We had been given many presents most were very practical but the one I liked best was a drawing that Nate did for us. It was a picture of the horses and our wagon. We also were given much of the food that was left over from the wedding reception so we ate a hearty meal and then retired to our wagon home. This time we cuddled together on the narrow bunks. They were designed for one person but I was not going to sleep in separate beds on the second night of my married life. That night I secretly applied more lard and then asked Robert to be gentle as he made love to me. It still hurt but I loved the closeness I felt as I let him use my body for his pleasure.

After Robert had fallen asleep, I lay next to him and reflected on how much my life had changed in the little over two months since I begged my Father to let me go to the church social having never been kissed to now being married and quite possibly pregnant if the amount of Roberts discharge was any indicator.

The next day, William, Roberts Poppa brought an older man to meet Robert and I. He kept looking me up and down and asked me if I could obey orders if he consented to allowing us to be part of his wagon train. Robert answered for me saying that I would do as I was told to do. I meekly nodded my head.

The wagon train was set to leave early Monday morning. People still respected the sabbath and everyone knew that, often while on the trail, Sundays would usually be just another day of travel. The Wagon Master's name was Earl and his plan was for us to travel to Independence, Kansas and then turn towards the South and take the Southern route. Earl told us that we would be able to travel to California and then follow another trail up the coast to the gold fields. The trip was longer but we would arrive about the time the Spring travelers would just be leaving. Earl claimed that we could cross the desert in the winter and not have the heat to deal with.

Robert wanted to see and spend time his buddy Nate so he invited him around to our wagon. I let the guys talk and went for a walk back to where my parents lived and after being warmly greeted was allowed to take a bath. The men often washed in the river but to maintain my modesty I chose to walk almost three miles back to where my parents lived. After a nice, warm bath and putting on the clean clothes I had brought with me, my Father offered to take me back to the staging ground. I sat next to him on the buggy seat and he placed his arm around me. It felt good to be close to him.

My Father kissed me and told me he loved me and then cautioned that I should always be a good wife and do as my husband asked. I giggled and went to the steps of the wagon. I entered to see two very drunk men. They had gotten a bottle of moonshine and were planning something.

Now, I liked Nate. He was polite and always telling jokes. He shoed horses for a living but he also had an artistic side. I had seen his drawings of horses and portraits of several people and they were so good they seemed lifelike. I wasn't sure that I liked him and my husband getting drunk together. I didn't say it but I am sure the men could tell by my actions that I was not pleased with them.

Robert asked Nate to "go check the shoes on the horses" while he talked to me. After Nate slipped past me to go outside. Robert asked me if I wanted a drink but I remembered how I had felt when my Father gave me a drink so I declined. Robert was very horny and was kissing me and feeling my breasts before he asked me to do him a little favor.

Robert asked me to let Nate see my body. I was angry and hurt. When the man I loved asked me this I immediately shouted "No!". Robert knew that I would not budge on this so he told me how Nate had never been with a woman and how he wanted to do a drawing of a partially dressed woman. My husband also admitted that he wanted Nate to know how lucky he was to be married to me. I loved the complements but I wasn't going to give myself to his friend. When I still refused, he played his ace and the rest of his hand. Robert asked me if I remembered my promise. We hadn't been together long enough to have many promises and I knew exactly what he was referring to. I had promised to do whatever he wanted sexually with no questions. If Robert wanted me to put his penis in my mouth I was prepared and even a little excited by the idea, I wasn't prepared to let his friend see, touch or have my body.

He also reminded me that I should respect his wishes. I wasn't sure that this was included in what I was supposed to do but I had promised, even though I had meant I would do it only for my husband. Robert seemed to read my mind and said I would be doing it for him because it would excite him. In a last-ditch effort, I told my husband that I would not redeem my promise to him tonight and that I would let Nate see my body. I hinted that maybe I would even let his friend touch a bit, if I did not have to have sex with his friend. I wasn't sure if I was happy, scared or angry, when he agreed.

I knew I was super fresh since I had just bathe and put on clean clothes and when Robert and Nate returned to the wagon, I sat them down on the bunk we used for our bed, and told them both, with much more authority than I felt, what I was willing to do for them. I told Nate that I was going to pose for him, one time, and that I would let him choose what I wore and how I posed as long as it wasn't too risqué. I playfully warned him that he would see my body but that I expected he would never breathe a word of this to anyone. After extracting his eager promise, I showed him the outfit I wore for my wedding night. Nate thought that would be fine and looked like he might begin drooling at any minute.

Robert wanted me to pose now but Nate and I decided that there was not sufficient room or light in the wagon for him to draw me. Nate told us that he knew a place deep in the woods where we would not be interrupted and the surroundings would create a perfect background. Nate said he would be back tomorrow mid-morning and asked me to wear the wedding set for him.

That night Robert was insatiable. He kept asking me questions about what I was willing to do for Nate. He asked me if I would let Nate see my breasts, and since the wedding set was so sheer, I agreed that he would see my breasts. Robert asked me if I would let his friend see my womanhood. I didn't think that was necessary but the post cards I had frequently looked at often showed the lady bits as a dark mass of hair so I guessed that if Robert was there, I would allow it.

The next day Nate arrived early and we walked over a mile into the woods. I had put my wedding nighty on under my dress and the place Nate had found was beautiful. It had a huge cottonwood tree that had fallen over many years ago and one of the large side branches made a nice place for me to recline for his drawing. Nate explained what he wanted and it made sense but then he didn't seem to know how to ask me to undress.

I stepped behind the trunk of the old tree which made a nice privacy screen. I could just see over the top of it so I could watch the men as I removed my clothes. Outside in the cool breeze I felt very exposed in the thin white outfit. I knew that this was about letting Nate see my body as much as being a model for Nate. Robert especially, wanted Nate to see my body. I know Nate wanted to see a nude woman but he was also genuinely excited about being able to do his drawing.

The men were deep in conversation when I stepped out from behind the tree, but they stopped and stared appreciatively as I walked to the limb and leaned against it. For a while I did not know what to do with my hands. I wanted to cover myself but that would have ruined what I had agreed to do. I tried letting them rest at my sides but I was afraid I would cover myself if I became any more nervous. I decided that for now I would hold them behind my back. I would not be so tempted to cover my private areas and the act of holding them behind my back would cause my breasts to stick out even more. Nate and Robert were next to me in a second and after much blushing and stuttering, Nate told me that Robert had told him to touch me as he posed me. I looked over at my husband and he had a look of absolute lust on his face. I smiled at Nate and told him that I was his to use for the next hour.

He carefully pulled back my top till my breasts were exposed and then covered one, leaving the other exposed. He then began to bend one of my legs into the position he wanted. Robert interjected that it would look better if I removed my panties. I expected this so when Nate agreed I slipped them off and handed them to my husband. I am sure parts of them were a bit damp. I returned to the pose I was in before and when Nate bent my one leg at the knee, I knew he would be seeing everything I had. He spent a good deal of time getting my top just right and touched my breast several times. Again, I expected this and just smiled at him as he continued to make minor adjustments.

Both men were hard as Robert got his pad and began to draw. I sat very still for well over and hour as Nate fussed with his drawing, erasing and redrawing little details. When I began to get sore, he let me move about. I didn't bother to dress because he had seen everything anyway. After our break he posed me again and his touches were more direct. He actually gave my nipple a little pinch. In a short while he announced that he was finished.

I hurried to where he stood and was shocked by what I saw. The drawing looked exactly like me and the expression he drew on my face was more seductive than I had ever been able to produce when I practiced in front of the mirror. The bad part was that he had focused on my lady bits and they were shown in graphic detail. I was shocked and excited at the same time. I knew that anyone who saw this would know that I was his model and that I had let him see all of me.

I told him that he couldn't show anyone because it looked so real and he took that as a compliment. He told me that he wanted to draw a copy of it for his use, I suspected that it was to masturbate to, but he said that he would deliver the original to me in the morning before we left as a thank you for letting him draw me. We walked back to the staging area with both men teasing me and telling me how beautiful I was. This didn't hurt my ego a bit.

We returned to the wagon and went inside to visit for a while. Robert talked about California and Nate talked about being an artist. After a while Robert and Nate said their goodbyes and Nate made to leave. Just before he opened the rear flap, I asked Nate to wait for just a second. With that I made my way past my husband in the crowded wagon and put my arms around Nate's neck and pulled him to me for a passionate kiss. I kissed him hard and even let our tongues become acquainted while I rubbed my body against his. I kissed him with as much passion as I had kissed Robert when we were dating and could feel his erection poking my lower belly. I stepped back and told him that I wanted him to remember me and then made my way back to the front of our little wagon.

Robert seemed upset after Nate had gone and I questioned him. He asked me why I had kissed Nate and I responded that he had let Nate touch my private areas and he would have let Nate have sex with me if I had agreed, so he should not be worried about a little kiss. I could tell he was angry with me and he told me that it was much harder to see me kissing Robert than it was to see him touching me. That night Robert fucked me, he didn't make love to me like he had before but he tried to subdue me with his penis, to reclaim me as his own. I had bathe earlier knowing that Robert would want to be intimate when we went to bed and I was looking forward to it because since losing my virginity tonight was the first night, I was not tender down there and I was looking forward to enjoying sex.

7 CHAPTER SEVEN

The next morning after the hard sex, twice, with Robert and having both his fingers and his penis up inside me, I was again a little sore, but I was a satisfied bride. Further, I felt a bit smug that I may have taught Robert a lesson and he would not try to let others see my body. There was movement the next morning even before the sun began to rise. Everyone was anxious to leave, Earl, the Wagon Master said he wanted to cover 25 miles the first day. Earl said the trail to Independence was heavily traveled and we would make good time.

Robert had our team harnessed and to my surprise there were four Percheron horses to pull the wagon instead of the two I had always seen when he came to visit me in the nearly empty wagon. Now, fully loaded he hitched all four horses to pull us to California. We had, by far, the most beautiful wagon and team. Some had 4 or 5 pair of oxen and others had mules or regular horses broke to the harness, to pull their wagons. The new white canvas that had been treated with linseed oil to make it waterproof was a beautiful sight. We had a total of twenty wagons, I counted, including ours. There were nineteen families because one family had two wagons. I should not say families because most of the wagons were just men headed to the gold fields. Usually two or three guys would go together to share the cost of the trip. I only counted four couples, including Robert and I. There were only four females as best I could count, four wives.

With 20 wagons Earl must have made $2000 because he had charged everyone a hundred dollars per wagon. Maybe only 1900 if the family with two wagons was given a discount. If I had known the terms of the agreement Robert and William had made with the wagon master, I may have refused to go. If I had known the terms before we were married, I may have refused that too. Earl did not have a wagon because it was agreed that he would take his meals with a different family each night and sleep under the stars or under a wagon if necessary. He had a small pack on his horse and a bedroll.

Most people used wagons they had or purchased lighter farm wagons rather than the Conestoga wagon so often depicted. The Conestoga freight hauling wagon was much too large and heavy for the trails, most were 4x10 or 12 with the box caulked and tarred so water would not get in when fording streams.

Of course, my father in law, William showed up with all his worldly possessions in a couple of carpet bags. I quickly learned that he would always have an excuse to ride in the wagon and I would be walking most of the way to California. I was wearing my regular drawers under my dress and since they didn't cover my woman parts I would feel the results of my husband's passion, the night before, slipping down my legs for the first several miles.

Earl was correct, the trail from St. Louis was a dirt road, it had been traveled enough that settlers and property owners along the trail often drug the road to make it smoother and filled ruts and holes to make it easy traveling. Earl had expected us to cover 25 miles but even with the good road, most of the travelers were not in shape to walk that much and the stock pulling the wagons was also not used to working that hard. At the end of the day we had covered only 15 miles and where we camped you could still see the lights of St. Louis from the nearby bluff.

The second and each successive day was about the same. We averaged about twenty miles a day on the good trail. Each day took a toll on our resources. The draft animals were suffering and needed rest. Robert was amorous for the first few days and we would sneak away into the woods after most had gone to sleep. Robert never lasted more than a few strokes so I would bend forward and he would relieve himself in my vagina. Some nights he would mount me after his father began to snore. As the number of days on the trail increased our love making decreased. Robert would fall asleep right after we ate and I would often do the same. The good news was that my monthly visitor did not arrive. With as much sperm as Robert had pumped into me, I expected that I was pregnant but one of the other women told me that it is not unusual to stop my periods when I was getting this much exercise. I wanted to have Robert's baby but being pregnant and trying to walk to California would not have been fun or wise.

That night was spent camping but because the trail had been used for many years, we often spent the night in a small town or near some local settlers' home. The first several days people mostly ignored us or came to us trying to sell us something. Often it was liquor and this often led to members of our train being too sick the next morning to travel well. In the city of Jefferson, a couple guys left their wagon to go into town and did not return. After an hour we were forced to leave them behind. They never did catch up to us.

8 CHAPTER EIGHT

The family with two wagons became friendly with us. It was a Father, Mother and a son, who was just a little younger than I was. The Father and the Son, whose name was Brad would each drive a wagon and the Mother would walk with me for most of the day. We would visit but later in the day her son would tie the reins of the horses and get down and walk with me, leading his wagon, so that his mother could ride. He often suggested that I ride with his mother but I always refused because their horses did not need the extra load and we had a perfectly good wagon that my Father in Law could have led as well.

Robert liked Brad and he would visit our wagon if he had time after making camp. Robert thought he was trying to befriend him but I am pretty sure he had a crush on me because his eyes always followed me while he was visiting with my husband. He was a sweet boy and I enjoyed the attention.

Each day we stopped several times to rest the ourselves and the animals. During these times us women would go into the woods, or if there were no trees, we would go over a hill or behind tall grass to relieve ourselves. The men would just go behind the wagons to pee and many times I would see a man peeing in the distance if I looked at the wrong time. It was during one of these rest stops that I noticed a man watching us from a distance. He was standing in the shadow's half way behind a tree with his penis out and touching himself. It's not like he could see anything because all of us women were wearing long dresses. We had all cut them to just below our knees to make walking easier but they covered everything and especially as far away as he was, I am sure he couldn't see our private parts. I didn't ever see the private's parts of the women and I was with them and usually squatting near them. Our dresses covered us while we peed and normal modesty caused us to turn away as we wiped ourselves.

The journey from St. Louis to Independence took us over three weeks to complete so during our travels we had stopped to bathe only twice and were all due for another bath when we arrived in Independence. We washed, usually daily, but bathing, which amounted to once a week and was usually conducted in a small creek that fed into the Missouri river that we were loosely following in our trek west, was a different story. We all went away from the wagons, carrying clean clothing, and found a private spot where we disrobed and washed ourselves in the usually cool water. When I saw the man this time, he was closer and openly masturbating, so I told the other women. Several of them began yelling at the man and he ran away back to the wagons. We were mostly covered in our underwear before the men from the wagon train came running to see what the commotion was all about.

The men openly chastised us for making such a scene, saying we acted like someone was trying to kill us, and promised to talk to the man. They acted like we were at fault as much, if not more than, the man who had invaded our privacy. Several of the men and the wagon master did go talk to the man when we returned to camp. There was shouting and a fight broke out when one of the married men attacked the man who had spied on us, but Earl broke up the fight. I thought he would be forced to leave our wagon train but he was allowed to stay with the promise that it would not happen again. It did seem that after learning that he had spied on us the other men avoided him. I felt kind of sorry for the man because he was just curious, like Nate had been, but I didn't mention that to anyone. That evening Robert and I slipped away from camp and he spent a lot of time asking me in great detail, what that guy had seen. He also asked what the other women in our group looked like naked.

Independence was a busy town and had a bath house. We all had baths with fresh hot water. Us women went together and helped each other and then the woman who owned the business helped the men in each of the three curtained off bathing areas. Our baths cost us two bits each which was a lot of money as many people didn't make that in a day but it was worth it. I am pretty sure the woman also offered other services in addition to the hot baths. My husband and William came back quickly but some of the other men, including the husband of the couple with the two wagons stayed much longer and I heard bits and pieces of conversations that indicated she provided more than hot bath water. The next day his wife seemed miffed but she did not say why and I was afraid to ask. Several days later she mused that she couldn't really blame her husband for evening the score but that Earl wasn't her fault and she didn't even enjoy it. When she saw the shock on my face, she immediately apologized saying that she was just prattling on and refused to explain, to me, what she was talking about.

We camped near Independence for an extra day and we purchased a few items that had been brought up the river, to merchants there, by barge. Even though we had only been traveling for three weeks it was time to replenish our supplies.

It began to rain that evening and the rain forced everyone to move inside their wagons early. Since Robert and his father had the day to rest, they were both in a randy mood. Robert wanted to have sex even before it was dark and when I said I would not since his Father was there, William piped up and said that he did not mind. I stood my ground and my husband was good natured about it but he kept rubbing my breasts and bottom every time he got a chance. Towards dark Robert told me to get ready for bed but when I went to hang a sheet for privacy, he pulled it down. I knew what he wanted. He wanted to show me off to his father like he had to, his friend, Nate.

Determined not to give his Father as much of a show as Nate had received, I let out a sigh and began removing my dress. Both Robert and William were watching intently when I removed the dress and reached for my night gown before removing my underclothes. Quick as a flash Robert grabbed the gown and held it out of my reach, saying that he would give it back when I was undressed. My underwear did not cover me very well and wrestling with my husband for the gown would have only given his father a better show so I relented and stripped off. This time I was not excited I was just embarrassed.

The men were excited, I could tell they were both hard, and Robert pulled me onto his lap and began kissing me as he fondled me on the outside of my gown, I liked the play but was self-conscious about having his Father for an audience. Even though I knew William was wide awake and listening to every sound, as soon as it was dark, I relented and let my husband push my gown up above my breasts and make love to me, twice. We had begun a crude form of birth control by having Robert pull out just before he came during the last couple weeks just to make sure I did not catch and then not be able to make the trip. However, that night I wrapped my legs around Robert when he was close and would not let him pull out until he had shot his sperm deep inside my vagina. This excited him so much that he did not lose his erection and he immediately wanted to go again. I am sure his father could hear the squishing sounds as his son pumped into me but I didn't care who heard us right then. My husband was excited and making love to me, his wife.

The trail past Independence was not nearly as good as the trail leading there. It was rougher and to make it worse the weather went from bad to worse. It rained for several day and then came a blizzard. This meant that we could not travel. We were a week out from Independence and the open plains of Kansas offered little protection from the storm. Everyone stayed inside their wagon and Earl chose to spend the night with the couple and their son who had the two wagons. I noticed that the husband and their son left the wagon and went for a walk leaving Earl with their wife and mother. I do not know why they left but they stayed gone for a couple hours. Maybe they visited another wagon but why would they do that when Earl was in their wagon.

The next day the weather broke and even though there were a few inches of snow on the ground, the skies were blue and the early snowfall began to melt. We traveled only a few miles that day because it was hard going and we came to a creek that was flooded and we would have to wait until it went down some to safely cross. Polly seemed nervous that Earl might try to spend the night in their wagon again but he chose the couple that was just the man and his wife, they were several wagons ahead of us but the next day I saw Earl leaving their wagon and he seemed really happy.

Again, being well rested and with little to do Robert was feeling amorous. Thankfully William gave us some privacy while he joined a card game with several of the fellow travelers. Robert was still obsessed with what the man may have seen when he spied on us. I told my husband truthfully that he did not see much but that I felt sorry for him. This got Robert going and he suggested that he would let the man come to visit and show him my body. I responded that I would not allow it in the strongest terms possible but it is hard to be very convincing when your husband is buried inside you and making you feel fantastic.

The next day Robert rode one of the Percheron across the small river and tied a rope to a tree to act as a guide and keep the horses from being pulled down stream. One by one the wagons made their way across. Sometimes the wagon would float and try to go down stream but the caulked and tarred wagon box kept things mostly dry. When the last wagon before our wagon began to cross, I noticed that it was the man who had spied on us and another older man. Their wagon was smaller and we later learned that it had not been made watertight. Almost as soon as they entered the river it began to sink and be pulled downstream against the guide rope.

Because the strong current of the river tried to pull the wagon under the rope it began to capsize the wagon.

Robert launched the Percheron into the stream and was able to catch a rope on their lead horses' collar and pull them to safety. When they emerged from the water on the other side Robert was hailed as a hero but everything in the small wagon was soaking wet and most of their food was ruined.

The Wagon Master allowed an hour for everyone to help them dry out and a fire was built to help the two men who had become soaked to warm up and put on dry clothes that they borrowed from the other travelers. We moved on and that night the men spread their wet possessions out in front of the fire and tried to salvage what they could. Clothing was dried but flour and sugar and many other essentials were ruined. Because they had lost so much Robert invited them to join us for our evening meal.

Even though our little group had been together for over a month I had never noticed these two men. The man who had spied on me was named Jacob and his partner was his Father, Paul. I learned that Jacob's Mother had died in childbirth and his Father had raised him. He was somewhere in age between Robert and me but had a birthmark that covered part of his face. In person he was a soft-spoken timid person and without addressing the reason he had been spying on the women, he made it clear he was going to California to get rich so that a woman would be interested in him even though he had a dark purple birthmark on his face. I made the usual sounds that he would find someone who loved him for who he was but I don't think anyone believed it.

9 CHAPTER NINE

We pushed hard for the next few days and the weather warmed so we made our average twenty miles per day. There were noticeably less towns and people since we left Independence. Things seemed to have settled down to a regular routine.

Today, I had gone to the outside of the circle of wagons to board the wagon, Just as I started to step up, I felt a powerful hand on my shoulder, preventing me from pulling myself up into the high seat. With his left hand on my shoulder, he used his right to rub and fondle my backside. I froze at first, and then looked over my shoulder to see Earl, the Wagon Master. I felt what he was doing and stated loudly for him to let me go. He just smiled and said, "Here let me give you a hand" while he pushed his strong fingers between my legs and lifted me with only my skirt between his fingers and my private parts. Only my husband and Nate had touched me there.

When he had me on the seat, he tipped his hat and turned to my Father -in-law, who was checking the harnesses, and politely said, "You need to have a talk with her, we should make it to the Osage valley and camp up against the high bluffs tonight. If she tries anything like that again, you can find your own way to California.

I was so shaken that I didn't know what to do. As we did most mornings, I would ride for the first couple hours and then William would ride, claiming his rheumatism was flaring and I would be forced to walk for the remainder of the day. Today we hadn't driven the team a mile before William climbed up beside me. I started to climb down but he told me to continue riding since this portion was smooth and slightly downhill.

Once he sat beside me, he asked what I had done to upset Earl. I blushed at the thought of telling another man what the Wagon Master had done. My Father-in-law repeated his question and to satisfy his curiosity I said that he had "accidentally" touched my bottom when he helped me into the wagon this morning. I expected that he would understand and maybe even side with me but instead he told me in a firm and gruff voice, "You're not a little girl anymore. Next time you don't complain…You hear me!!"

Next time! I had hoped that by making a SCENE, there would not be a next time.

We made good time into the Osage valley, we followed the small river along between the high bluffs. The trail was narrow and we crossed the small river at least a dozen times because the river sometimes flowed right next to the bluff, forcing us to the other side. Fortunately, the water was very low and we barely got our boots wet. Since I had cut the lower part of my dress off, almost to my knees, to make for easier walking I could cross by holding my dress up a bit and never got wet.

We found a great camping area, protected from the north winds by a high bluff with a large meadow to graze the livestock. Earl no longer seemed angry with me and instructed Robert to park our wagon up against a willow thicket to insure we had a warm camping spot.

The next morning Earl announced that the stock needed rest and that a hunting party should be formed to see if they could bag a couple deer for our reserves. He put my husband in charge of half a dozen men and sent them hunting. Earl stayed back along with William and a few less able-bodied others to look after the stock as they grazed.

No sooner than the hunting party left Earl called William aside and they spoke quietly. I couldn't hear the conversation but after a few minutes my father in law said, "Yes Sir" and walked back to our wagon. He looked me in the eye and told me to go to the other side of the wagon and to wait there for Earl to help me. I started to complain that we were not going anywhere, the team was not even hooked up, but I was told to do what he said and not to make a scene or there will be serious trouble.

I walked to the back side of the wagon between the willow bushes and our wagon and stood there looking across the front of our wagon where we normally sat. I heard him this time as his step's broke small twigs. I did not look his way and pretended to be looking into the circle of wagons. I almost jumped when William stepped forward on the other side of the wagon and was looking directly at me. He admonished me again, Don't Complain! and then stood there watching.

It was about then I felt Earl standing very close behind me. He put his hands on my sides and moved then up and down, when he got to my breasts, he cupped them from behind me and stage whispered across the wagon to William, "She's got a pretty decent body, your boy did good getting her". He then raised the back of my dress and rubbed his hands over my drawer clad behind. "Hold your dress up woman" he said. With trembling hands, I gripped the coarse cloth and held it. "Higher woman", he said, so I gently tugged it higher. I felt his rough hand push my drawers down and then he pushed on the back of one knee like I was a horse, forcing me to raise my leg and let him slip the panty over my foot. Earl then pushed my legs further apart with his foot. I repositioned myself and with my legs apart I was forced to lean slightly forward against the wagon. I was completely bare down there and he could see everything I had. I felt his hands sliding over my butt and prodding between my legs. When his big finger touched my womanhood, I let out a small gasp. Quickly William, who was still on the other side of the wagon looking at me, scolded me, telling me to stay quiet. I knew I should protest but both of these men were in positions of authority and I was afraid to upset them.

I had never felt the feelings that coursed through my body as this gruff man touched my private parts while my father in law watched and made sure I cooperated. It was only a bit over a month ago that I gave my body to my husband, for the first time, and now I was standing passively allowing the Wagon Master his pleasure.

He continued to touch me down there and to force his finger into my body. I was too embarrassed to look at him but soon caught myself gently rocking on his thick finger. He pulled his finger from between my legs and left me standing there. With his hand gone I felt the chill of the cool breeze on my now damp womanhood. I heard him unbuttoning his trousers as he prepared to enter me. In a gruff voice he told me to bend over more, so I silently leaned forward, onto my forearms, against the wagon. I knew without a doubt what was about to happen and, so far, I had not resisted.

I looked across the wagon, directly into William's eyes. He could not see my exposed lower body but it was obvious what the wagon master was doing to me. His facial expressions showed the lust he too was feeling. I tuned out what Earl was doing to me and focused on the expressions of lust in my Father in law's face as he watched me being used. I felt Earl move behind me and press his bare cock against the crack of my bottom. His cock felt hot against my now slightly chilled skin. Earl reached around me and unbuttoned my dress. I had not bound my breasts, thinking that since we would be in camp today, I could forgo that discomfort.

The Wagon master opened my dress, exposing my breasts to my father in law, and began to squeeze them as he humped against my back side trying to find the opening of my womanhood with his hard cock. Just as the tip of his cock was getting close, the sound of voices caused him to stop. As he hurriedly refastened his trousers, I let my dress fall to the ground and buttoned the top of my dress. There was no time to replace my drawers and the wagon master grinned as he tucked my panties into his pocket, telling me that he would return them later.

10 CHAPTER TEN

The hunting party had come across a large buck with his antlers caught in a tree. They easily dispatched him and had returned quickly with a good supply of meat.

With the hunting complete, the Wagon Master suggested we camp for another day to let the stock rest. The mood around the camp was a time of celebration, as we took our evening meal, families visited with the other members that, even though part of the same group, they had seldom talked. No sooner than the meal was complete, the temperature began to drop quickly and everyone hurried to make sleeping places in their wagons.

The wagons were in a loose circle, not so much for security but it provided a corral for the livestock. The wagon directly in front of us was another young couple. They were in their twenties and were still childless. The wife, Molly, and I had chatted a few times and she made it clear that she did not like Earl. She would not tell me why but told me that I would soon learn. I noticed that Earl chose to spend the night in the wagon with Molly and her husband.

Even with only the three of us in a 4x12 area, with the bath tub, and boxes everywhere, there was little room. William told us to make a pallet on top of the boxes and he would sleep on top of the bunk. We left our underclothes on and cuddled under the quilts I had brought with us. Robert was feeling amorous and since it had been several days since I had done my wifely duty, I was willing to let him, if we could be quiet and not wake his Poppa.

He was insistent the I remove everything this time and I did so under the blankets. As I lay on my back, waiting for my husband to mount me I looked up and noticed my father-in-law peering down from his sleeping place above us. I gave a shriek and quickly covered my breasts that had become exposed as I waited for my husband to remove his pants.

"Your Father can see us!" I complained, as I huddled under the covers. "Well so what, we're married." My clueless husband replied, like this was no big deal.

About that time, William interjected, "You would think she was still a virgin by the way she acts. Hell, she about pissed Earl off today, acting like she didn't know her place."

My husband asked me what I had done and I defensively told him that Earl had tried to take liberties with me. He chuckled and told me that William was correct, I needed to grow up and not complain if other men found me attractive.

I honestly told him that I didn't know if I could do that because he and Nate were the only men who had ever seen me naked and that I wasn't used to this. He grinned and told me he knew what I needed.

He pulled the quilts off of me and the sudden rush of cold air almost took my breath away. I looked up and thankfully William was not to be seen. My thankfulness was short lived because his next words were, "Hey Poppa, take a look."
Williams face quickly appeared from the bunk above, he was looking straight down at my nude body and was barely three feet above me. I covered myself with one arm across my breasts and my other hand covering my coochie while I tightly crossed my legs.

I was so embarrassed that I do not even remember the cold; I suddenly felt hot. I knew not to disobey my husband so I lay there and let his dad see parts of me he shouldn't. This felt different than when Nate saw my body and I was not excited.

"Very nice son, how about I see all of her" he said and my husband quietly instructed me to "Let Poppa see you". When I hesitated, he gently lifted the arm covering my breasts and moved it aside, exposing my breasts to his Poppa. I know he had seen them when Earl played with me, but this was different.

Because the wagons only had a canvas top just about everything said inside, could be heard outside. My husband removed the hand covering my pubic hair and then touched the inside of my knee, indicating he wanted me to open my legs. I did as instructed and was in full view of my Father in Law. Prior to tonight, only my husband and his friend Nate had seen me this exposed. Well I guess Earl had seen most of me, but even my own father had not seen me nude since I was a baby.

My husband gently raised my knees and opened my legs as wide as they would go. I am sure I looked like a wanton slut as William continued to stare at me. From his position, I was sure, he could see right up inside me. I was so embarrassed that there were tears in my eyes.

I had my eyes closed but I soon heard the sounds of William masturbating to the sight of my body. His son climbed on top of me and while thankful for the fact he covered much of my body, I was embarrassed at how loud the sounds of our love making sounded and by the moans that I could not suppress. My husband may have suggested this for my benefit but shot his seed into my body quicker than ever before.

Clearly my husband did not care if other men saw what was supposed to be only his. He let his own Father see me nude and as such had instructed me not to resist Earl's advances. The next day one of the few other wives was at the stream filling their water buckets and asked me if the Earl had "gotten his" from me yet. I blushed brightly but now understood the little comments other women had been making. The Wagon Master planned to sample each of the women in our group. It was much later that I learned that it had been a condition of being allowed to bring the me on this long and dangerous journey. My husband, and apparently a few of the other men had agreed to "Look the other way" if the Wagon Master "Had a bit of fun with their wives."

11 CHAPTER ELEVEN

The next night my husband told me that Earl would come by after everyone had gone to sleep to "Take me for a walk" and told me that I should do what he says. Robert acted like it was no big deal, like maybe Earl was going to ask me to mend a shirt for him. I knew what Earl would want to do and I couldn't believe my husband knew and had agreed to what the Wagon Master would want me to do. I was a bit miffed but after I cooled off I decided that since my husband wanted me to do this, I would not put up a fuss. I had almost dozed off when I heard Earl whisper at the back flap of the wagon, "Anybody still awake?" I knew that his request was meant for me, so I buttoned my coat and moved past my husband and his Poppa. I quietly slipped out the back of the wagon, to meet Earl.

Earl motioned with a finger to his lips for me to be quiet and then took my hand and lead me away from the wagons. At first, he just held my hand but when we were out of sight, he put his arm around me, like a lover, trying to keep me from the cold night air. We stopped behind a willow thicket and he kissed me with passion. My husband is a good kisser, but Earl was even better. Even though I was not attracted to Earl, I found myself enjoying his kisses. They were different than the kisses my husband gave me. Earl lead me to a low hanging branch and had me lean against it. Like when he came behind me at the wagon, I could feel him pressing against me from behind. This time, however, he took his time. First, his hand found his way inside my coat and felt my breasts for a long time. Then he told me to lift my coat so he could, "Get to the good parts."

I had a surprise for Earl. Since my husband wanted me to do this, I decided that there was no point in making it difficult for Earl to undress me. I would do what he, and apparently my husband, obviously wanted me to do. I had decided to make it easy for him.

I had just worn a loose camisole without a petticoat under the exterior coat I was wearing. When I unbuttoned the coat and raised it, Earl saw my bare woman parts and my bare bottom, in the moonlight. He seemed to appreciate it and began repeating "You a good girl" over and over, as he worked his rough, and initially somewhat cold, fingers into my vagina.

This time I cooperated fully and pushed back onto his finger as I spread my legs a bit wider. I rocked on his fingers and the naughtiness of what I was doing caused me to get a warm and tingly feeling all inside me.

Earl dropped his pants and I suddenly felt his bare manhood poking my backside. I briefly had the sobering thought, that he could make me pregnant, but I wanted that tingly feeling to return so I pushed my bottom back toward Earl's cock. I used my fingers to open my hairy hole so Earl's cock could enter me.

My husband had sometimes done me this way when we would sneak off to have sex. Earl's cock was a lot thicker than my husband's and where my husband's cock seemed to be pointed, Earl's was thicker and blunt. This time, we were not rushed and Earls cock felt wonderful as he pushed into me from behind. After last night when my husband finished before I could even begin to enjoy what he was doing, I was soon panting like a dog while Earl continued his assault on my vagina. The warm feeling was back and I was moving with Earl to make it feel even better. Earl must have lasted ten times longer than my husband ever did and I welcomed his seed when he grunted and pushed his cock as deep as it would go inside me.

When Earl pulled out, I relaxed and turned to face him as he began to rebutton his pants. My coat was wide open but my camisole had fallen down to cover me. I untied the four little ties holding the camisole closed and opened it to let my new lover see my front as I faced him. I leaned back, on to the low hanging limb, and opened my legs so he could see between my legs.

Earl stopped what he was doing and again pulled his now soft cock out of his pants. He stepped between my legs and began kissing me and touching me everywhere. He wasn't getting hard so he said we had better get back to camp. He told me that next time he would spend all night with me in the wagon and if it was crowded Robert and William could find another place to sleep. I now knew what Earl had been doing. He had used the other wives all night and the husbands would leave so they did not have to watch Earl use their wife.

My plan to not wear underwear was good for easy access and felt sexy on our walk but now that my vagina was flooded with a huge amount of his sperm. It was not as fun feeling the sperm slowly drip down my thighs as we walked back to the wagons.

When I returned to the wagon, Earl gave me a kiss and then again motioned for me to stay quiet as I climbed back into our wagon. I blushed bright red when both my husband and William were up and waiting for my return. The inside of the wagon was very dark and since I could only vaguely make out their shapes, I knew they could not see my embarrassment or the evidence of what I had done.

I thought nothing would be said as I had done what was expected of me but William began to question me immediately. He was blunt and asked me to tell them what had happened. I couldn't at first as I sat there with my coat on but finally blurted out, "I did what you wanted me to do". He said "What's that." and I said "You know.... what he tried to do the other day." My husband, whispered, "Did you let him inside you?" I was suddenly unsure if I had done the right thing. I thought I was sure they had wanted me to let Earl have my body, but now I wasn't sure. He repeated the question and I looked down again, fearful I may have ruined my marriage. and nodded my head slightly. My husband gave a hearty laugh and pulled me to him, giving me, what was to that point, one of the most passionate kisses of our marriage. I was so relieved that I hadn't ruined my marriage that I giggled too.

Their questions didn't stop until I had told them exactly what Earl and I had done in great detail. I even told them how I surprised Earl, sans underwear, and how it had backfired on me by allowing his seed to drip down my leg on the walk home. Almost in unison they both said, "I want to see that." Of course, I refused and told them there was no way I was going to defile myself, even more, by showing them the proof of my meeting. William said that I should show them so that if Earl tried to say I hadn't lived up to their agreement, they would know, for sure, that he was lying. I still refused saying that there was nothing to see in the dark wagon and with that William lit a candle. Matches were precious so wasting one to light a candle was an impulsive action. Knowing how serious they were about seeing between my legs, I moved my hands away from my kitty and took off my coat. I sat there in only my thin camisole till my husband raised the camisole and pushed my knees apart allowing them to both see my well used womanhood.

After they had their fill of looking, I reached into my rag bag and used one of the flannel pads, I had sewn years ago, to clean my legs and vagina. Yes, my husband made love to me, with Earls seed still inside me, while his father watched from his bed above. Growing up, I had been lectured, frequently by teachers at church and my mother, that a woman should only do her wifely duties when she absolutely had to and then I should do it in a dark bedroom with as little emotion as possible. Here I was with two men's sperm inside my body and an audience, as I preformed my wifely duties. Tonight, I raised my legs a bit higher, to allow my husband even deeper into my body and let myself moan openly as my husband fucked me. I was beginning to enjoy this thing called sex.

12 CHAPTER TWELVE

The next morning, we were awakened by shouting. William and Robert dressed quickly and went out to see what all the commotion was about. I sat up and immediately felt a large amount of, Earls as well as my husband's, sperm slip from my vagina. I quickly found a pair of underpants and stuffed a period pad inside to catch their offerings. I was a bit sore but it was a good type of sore.

Earl had quietly taken his horse and left the camp in the predawn hours. There were many discussions as to whether he had gone ahead to scout or if indeed he had left the wagon train and disappeared. It didn't take long to determine that his tracks went back toward St. Louis and we had been abandoned.
The men met for several hours and about half of the group decided to return to St Louis with the faint hope of finding Earl and getting their money back. They vowed to try again in the spring.

The other half were determined to continue on, even though they had never been on this trail before. With winter fast approaching, they felt that every day they traveled they would be closer to the California Gold. Among the ones choosing to continue on was Polly and her family, as well as the wagon with Brad and his Father. Since we were the only family that decided to stay where we were, we told those that planned to continue on, that we would post a sign on the main trail pointing to where we would stay, in case they were forced to turn back.

Robert and William decided that we would not return to St Louis because we had sold everything there, but they felt that leaving the protection of the forest and stream would also be unwise. We opted to find a place to settle in for the winter and then we could leave in the spring, with a five- or six-week head start on the others.

The following morning our wagon train split into two smaller wagon trains and headed off in opposite directions. We were left alone to fend for ourselves till spring, when we would most likely meet other travelers and join them on their trek to California.

Later that morning my husband saddled one of the horses and set out to find a comfortable place for us to spend the winter. He left William with me, promising to be back before dark. I used the time to heat water over the fire to wash the, now crusty, cum from the hair between my legs and give myself a sponge bath. I then used the hot water to wash our clothes. I had been somewhat shy about washing and hanging my under things to dry when other men would see them. Now that we were alone, William had seen my underwear and more, so I had no worries.

William gathered a large pile of firewood and after a lunch of venison and wild potatoes we sat and talked. He complemented me for letting Earl "enjoy himself" as he tactfully put it, and told me that I was now starting to understand the real world. I was blushing but I liked finally having his approval. He suggested that he would like to see my nude body, in the daylight, claiming that I was mostly in the shadows, when he watched my husband and I make love last night.

He put me on the spot because this was not sanctioned by my husband and even though I knew he had seen me naked, this was different. I wasn't sure my husband would approve. Apparently, he wasn't sure he would approve either because he chose to bring it up when my husband was not nearby.

I also did not want to lose my Father-in-Laws approval. I could tell he was getting angry as I kept dodging his suggestions. I decided that since he had seen me nude, having sex and had even masturbated while looking at me, it would be okay if he saw me undressed again. I told William that I would show him what he wanted to see, but he had to promise that he would not touch me. He readily agreed so we went inside the wagon. In the daylight, the white canvas afforded a bit of privacy, but let all of the light in. Not that there was another human being anywhere near us, it just felt more comfortable to take my clothes off, inside the wagon. It had the added bonus of being several degrees warmer inside.

I again reminded William of his promise not to touch and began removing my clothes. This time I unbuttoned my dress slowly, while I watched my Father-in-Law's face, as he anticipated seeing my body. When I was down to my panties and a camisole William stopped me and told me that he wanted to look at me for a while. I could see the bulge in his pants and knew I had caused it. He had me bare my breasts next and play with my nipples. I had often done that, but before, it was in private.

He then asked me if I had enjoyed what Earl did to me. I avoided his question and asked him if I should remove my panties. He was breathing hard and stared as I slowly untied the panties and removed them. I was glad I had washed the evidence from last night away as I stood before my husband's Father, totally nude.

He had me pose for him, which was both embarrassing and exciting at the same time. Knowing he was looking at my bottom when he had me turn around, gave me a bit of a tingle. I started to get dressed and he firmly stated that he wasn't done. His voice scared me a bit, but he volunteered that he would not touch. He just wanted to get a good look. I followed his requests which included shaking my bare breasts and laying down, facing him and opening my legs like I did for his son.

He had pulled his cock out and was stroking himself as he looked at my body. While I knew he masturbated it was only from hearing him in the dark wagon. This was the first time I saw his manhood. It was longer than his son's but also uncut and pointed. He was kneeling between my legs, and getting close to his own release when he asked the same question, about Earl, again. This time I told him the truth, "Yes! I liked it a lot" I then raised my legs like I had for his son the night before and opened myself like I had for Earl. William came hard shooting his cum all over my coochie and belly. I am glad I was laying because what I was doing was so taboo that I know my legs would not have held me up. I felt good, knowing I had made him cum.

By time Robert returned, that evening, it was almost dark. He believed that we could travel for about two days and then move across the prairie to a valley he had found that would provide shelter for us as well as being only a few miles from the main trail.

That night, I was feeling devious. Maybe, what I had done with my husband's father, earlier, let me feel that way. I made sure that several of the buttons on the front of my dress, accidentally on purpose, came undone and I would fold it open and let William see my breasts when Robert wasn't looking. As soon as we went into the wagon, Robert lay down and instantly fell asleep. William acted like he was going to leave the wagon and as he passed me, he reached out and cupped my breast. He put his finger to his lips, to silence me, and then stood in front of me for several minutes with his hand inside the front of my dress touching my bare breasts. I could feel his hardness poking me in my belly but I refused to touch him. His touch was not unpleasant but my fear of Robert catching us cause me to not enjoy what was happening, as much as I had hoped I would.

The next morning, with the horses harnessed, we began to travel again but not before William whispered into my ear that he wanted me to show him my "Cunt". That was a coarse term for my vagina and I had always used the proper term or referred to it as my "Womanhood, Lady Bits, Coochie or in front of Emily or my sisters I would call it my Kitty or even my Pussy but never my Twat or Cunt.
His crude request was both a turn off and a bit exciting at the same time. I stood inside the wagon just behind the driver's seat and hiked my dress up. After I had removed my drawers I whispered to William to, "Turn around and look at my Cunt". I said it, I said Cunt and I think it shocked him. I stood there with my dress held high with one foot on a box and my womanhood fully on display only a couple feet from his face. When he reached for me, I jerked back and quickly replaced my drawers and went to assist my husband as we broke camp.

From then on William would playfully grab me when Robert wasn't looking.   I was still not keen on Robert fondling me or making love to me with his Father near, but I found I liked making it look like I accidentally was letting William see my body while his son petted me.

It took us three days till we were in the secluded valley my husband had located. It only took a couple days to get there but we had to cut down several trees to locate the wagon against a stony bluff that had a small cave. When the wagon was set there was a ten-foot space between the wagon and the mouth of the cave. The men spend several days building walls and a roof. We moved everything from the wagon and set the stove and the bathtub up in the new room. With everything in place, we entered through the new room, but we could turn left into the cave, which upon inspection had probably used for shelter, by Indians, for centuries. If we turned right, we were in the new cabin between the cave and the wagon. One the far side of the room, there was a set of steps into the back of the wagon.

This gave Robert and I more privacy when we slept in the wagon and William built a bed in the cave. The guys built a long and wide bench, that could double as a table or bed if the weather got too cold, and placed it near the stove in the center section. Water was close in the stream so the first night I warmed water then hung a blanket for my privacy with the intent of taking a nice long hot bath. I was disappointed when Robert stripped off and climbed into the tub. He had me wash his back and hair which he claimed was almost as good as sex. When he finished William took his place. He showed no modesty and took his clothes off in front of Robert and me. I blushed and turned away but William chastised me saying that it didn't matter because I was married and I would see him when I washed his back and his hair. I looked to my husband for support but his response was that I "HAD" to wash his dad's back because it felt so good.

Even though the water was becoming gray his penis poked up above the water and as I scrubbed his back. He was hard and it stuck several inches above the water. When Robert went into the wagon, William intentionally dropped the soap between his legs and smiled at me, daring me to reach for it. I grinned and reached between his legs, giving his manhood a couple quick strokes before retrieving the bar of lye soap and beginning on his hair. My heart was pounding so hard I thought I might pass out. Williams penis was only the second one I had, intentionally, felt in my entire life. I never saw Nate's and I never touched Earl's, with my hand, so even though I only touched William briefly, it was very exciting.

After William was done, the water was so dirty and cool that I refused to bathe in it. I drained the tub and refilled the tub with warm, no hot, water from the stove. When I was ready to undress and get in the tub, both men were sitting on the table watching me. I suggested that I would put up a blanket and they threatened to take it down so I did the next best thing. I started disrobing and removed my dress, as I stood before them with only my long camisole and drawers on. The guys were grinning thinking that they would get a sexy show but I snubbed the lantern and quickly removed my underwear and slipped into the tub. By time they were able to relight the lantern I was in the tub and with only the tops of my breasts exposed. They liked seeing my breasts but it was not uncommon to see a woman nursing her baby. Some women tried to cover themselves but many women, especially during the summer months or if the child was older, would just open their dress and pull out a breast so I was not overly embarrassed if my husband let his Poppa see my breasts. I may have even raised up and let more of my breasts be exposed a few times to tease both of them. They threatened to wait until I got out but after a while William went to the cave to sleep and Robert washed my back and hair. I had to admit it felt heavenly and probably better than the sex we had most of the time.

We had been there a few days when Robert took a horse back to the main trail and posted a sign advertising Hot Baths for 50 Cents. I did not expect anyone would see the sign until Spring. When Robert and I would go into the wagon he would whisper that he wanted me to wash the men's backs and let them do whatever they wanted to me. Of course, I refused and acted angry but deep down wondered what it would be like if a man came for a hot bath. Either way I was sure that no one would be traveling the trail until spring and by then we would be on our way to California.

Robert seemed to get excited thinking about letting other men see me. He had let his friend Nate see everything and he had agreed to let Earl have me as partial payment for our trip to California. I am pretty sure he knew that his Poppa was taking liberties with me but chose to look the other way. The reason I believe he knew is because on nights where William would cop a few feels or I would, accidentally on purpose, let his see more than he should, my husband was extra randy when we went to bed.

On Friday night Robert was extra horny and kept trying to feel me up in front of his Father. He and his Poppa/Father had gone hunting and bagged a huge Buffalo. We would have meat for the entire winter from this one animal. When William went outside to get more firewood, I asked him why he was doing stuff when his Poppa could see. He told me that his Father's birthday was in two days and wanted me to let his Poppa see my body so that he had something new to think about when he masturbated.

I teased back that maybe I would let his Father see more when we all took our baths tomorrow night and then to tease my husband, I added that I should help William wash his front as well as his back. I thought I was being silly but Robert was instantly obsessed with the idea saying that "Making sure he was really clean "would be the hottest thing ever. I wasn't sure how I was going to get myself out of this one. I had already touched William's cock, so I knew he would not object, but it seemed weird to do anything in front of my husband.

That night after we all went to bed, Robert and I negotiated what I would do. Even though I knew William would welcome me touching his penis I pretended that it would be hard for me to do and to make it easier for me I got Robert to agree to leave us alone "To make William more comfortable". I am pretty sure William could have cared less if his son was in the room as long as I rubbed his cock for him. I told Robert that he could secretly watch through the cracks in the logs. There were several places that the mud we used to chink the logs had dried out and was loose or missing. I gave up my top by agreeing that I would wash William with my breasts exposed. We agreed that I could tell William there would be no touching but my husband told me that I was not to try to stop his Poppa if he tried to touch my breasts.

The best part of negotiating with my husband for nearly two hours is that he kissed and fingered me for the entire time and mounted me three times with the last time lasting long enough for me to get that wonderful feeling down there. Each time Robert pulled out and came on my belly to help prevent pregnancy.

Our isolated camping spot seemed as if we were the only people on earth and while we stayed busy during the day with the men working on the cabin and me cooking, cleaning and preparing for the evening baths, it was a very relaxed day. I had the men bring a large wooden barrel into the cabin and then carried buckets of water from the little creek till both the stove and the barrel were full of water. When the men were busy, I filled a basin and washed myself, especially between my legs and under my arms. Even though Robert had not shot any sperm inside me last night there was dried sperm in my pubic hair and I had a strong womanly smell. I anticipated that no one would see between my legs until I had taken my bath but I felt sexier when I was fresh down there. Tonight, I wanted to be very sexy when I helped William bathe. What I was about to do did not seem that bad because I knew that no one would ever know what happened because we were alone in this little valley.

That night we had a huge meal of roasted buffalo, potatoes, and a salad made with watercress I found growing in the spring. I also made bread for the first time since we began traveling. My mother had taught me many years ago but when we were traveling there was never time to actually make it. The mood was jovial as we ate and complimented William on his upcoming birthday. When we had finished our meal and had a hot cup of coffee, I suggested that we start our baths and that since tonight was Williams birthday celebration he be allowed to go first. William liked that and I volunteered that I would be happy to wash his back. My father in law remembered me touching his penis last week and began to remove his clothes even before I had the tub filled with hot water from the stove.

When William was distracted, I motioned for my husband to leave. I could tell he was disappointed but grabbed his coat and made comment about cutting some more firewood.

William was already hard when he eased himself into the hot water but I teased him more by removing my top. When he asked if I was going to join him in the tub, I told him that it was just so I would not get my clothes wet while I washed his back and hair and extracted a promise that he would not try to touch me.

He agreed but his eyes were glued to my breasts. I was positive that his son was watching my every move through a crack in the logs so I made sure I played to where I expected he was watching from. I continued to tease William by asking him if he liked seeing my breasts. He was almost drooling as he nodded and said yes. On an impulse I teased him more and asked if there was anywhere else, he wanted to see for his birthday. This time his voice was almost a croaking sound as he looked at my skirt and whispered, "Your Cunt".

I knew Robert would be thrilled for me to let his Father see my body so I stood near the tub and dropped my skirt and drawers in one smooth motion. I stood next to the tub, just out of his reach and again extracted a promise not to touch.

I took my time washing William's back and hair and there were times my breasts were within inches of his face. His eyes remained glued to my tits as they moved and jiggled while I scrubbed his body. Without being asked I moved to his front and began washing the coarse hair on his chest. We were now face to face as I knelt next to the tub and scrubbed his chest. Without breaking eye contact I reached between his legs and grasped his erect cock. William placed his arms on the sides of the tub to give me full access to his penis. I fondled him above and below the water, feeling his balls and length of his shaft. When his breathing became labored, I stopped and washed his legs until his breathing returned to normal. I carefully cleaned the foreskin of his penis like I had seen Robert do to himself when he washed himself. William was very hard and he was both slightly longer and a bit thicker than his son. I again looked directly into his eyes as I stroked him slowly towards his climax. I realized that my bare breast was touching his arm but only leaned against his hand more as he got closer. When William came, he grabbed my boob as I pumped five or six big spurts of cum from his penis. With his hand still on my breast I leaned close and hugged him, wishing him a happy birthday.

13 CHAPTER THIRTEEN

William made himself ready for bed and went to the cave about the time Robert came in. I noticed he did not bring in any firewood. Of course, I washed his back and hair but then he sat back with his arms on the edge of the tub and requested the same treatment his Poppa had received. I reenacted what I had done for his Poppa and predictably my husband shot his sperm, almost immediately. Having just had his Father's penis in my hand, less than an hour before, I could tell for sure that my husband was smaller than his Poppa. When we went to bed, he had me tell him what I had done to his Poppa but also made me admit that I had enjoyed making his Poppa cum.

I had been making hardtack for the last couple of days because the stove's warming oven was just the right temperature. Robert said that if anyone did stop on their travels, they would pay handsomely for hardtack to eat as they continued along the trail. He also said they would pay handsomely for me to give them a bath and sexual relief, but I quickly informed him that I was not a whore, and that I did what I did for him, only because I loved him.

The next morning, I awoke before my husband and got up to stoke the fire and make coffee. When the coffee was ready, I brought two cups back to the wagon and climbed in next to my husband. I teasingly stroked his penis as I closed my eyes and sipped the warm liquid. I liked having our own home, even if it was partially cave and wagon. I knew that after last night I would be expected to provide relief for Robert's father but the thought no longer scared me, in fact, it made me a little warm down below. After all, I enjoyed the feeling of power if gave me to see how bad he wanted to see my body and feel my touch.

Our early morning cuddle session was interrupted by someone yelling "Hello the house!!" It was a frontier custom not to walk up to a strange house without alerting the owners, to prevent being shot at. We scrambled for our clothes and got to the door at the same time William did. William stayed back and held a gun while Robert opened the door to see who was approaching.

It was our friends from the Wagon train, Polly, John and their teenaged son Brad. The had chosen to go on with nine other wagons to California. Without a Wagon Master patience was thin and two of the wagons turned around after a week or so and tried to return to Independence. We never learned if they were able to cross the river safely. The remaining wagons moved faster, by abusing their horses or oxen, leaving John and Polly and their two wagons behind. John had no problem following their trail but while trying to move along a small canyon after a fall snow storm the wagon Brad was driving slid off the edge of the trail and tumbled down into the canyon destroying one wagon and killing one of their best horses.

The worst part was that Brad's foot had been badly crushed. John had collected a few of the more valuable things from the wagon but the wagon was overloaded. They turned back towards Independ-ence to find a Doctor but with Brad unable to help and seeming to get worse they had made poor time. The day before, just before nightfall, they had seen Robert's sign offering hot baths. While not sure if it was Robert and Katie, the green letters were the same color that he had painted his fancy wagon. They hoped they could leave a few of their possessions there and possibly get Robert to transport Brad back to Independence, where he could get medical attention, in his fancy wagon.

The family looked totally defeated. They had not stopped to bathed in what was now almost a month. They were exhausted and the parents looked afraid because Brad's swollen foot could easily become fatal. We welcomed them with open arms and the men quickly formulated a plan for Brad and Polly to go with Robert to Independence in our wagon, while John stored some of their possessions in our cave and then followed behind in a couple days after the horses were allowed to recover.

The men helped Brad into the cabin and I prepared a large bucket of warm water and salts to help reduce the swelling in his foot. He was feverish and went from being chilled to being so warm he would throw off his covers. His spirits were good and he smiled at me like a love-sick boy.

The men removed our wagon from the side of the cabin and covered the hole with a canvas and some logs. I would have to sleep in the cabin on the table while Robert was away. It was decided that Robert and Polly would leave at first light in the morning so I hung a couple blankets around the tub for privacy and prepared a bath for the family that smelled as bad as they looked. John went first and I let his wife help him as I tended to getting the mid-day meal on.

Everyone, including Brad, decided that he would feel better if he had a bath so after lunch Polly and I helped him into the curtained off area. Brad did not want to undress in front of his Mother so she asked if I would help him into the tub. I helped him remove his clothes and when I removed his pants, he was semi hard. He blushed and told me that is why he didn't want his mother to see him nude. I teased him that he had nothing to be ashamed of and he beamed at my compliment. While Polly and the men were moving items from their wagon to the cave, he admitted that he had never been with a woman and told me that he knew he might die from his injuries. He looked straight at me and told me he wished he could be with a woman before he dies.

Even though he hadn't specifically asked me for sex I too knew that he would likely die before he reached Independence and even if he did make it there was a good chance he could not be saved. I began washing Brad's body. First his back and his hair which, from the sounds he made, he greatly enjoyed. His erection poked up from the water like an angry serpent and I could tell it was the largest I had ever seen. I was not sure the rest of my plan would work so I began washing Brad's front.

Brad was so excited that he was actually quivering and I was sure it was not from the infection. I used a small hand towel to dry his hands and then placed one under my shirt and onto my bare breast while I gently stroked his hard penis. He began to moan loudly and I didn't want his parents to hear so I kissed him firmly on the lips while I made him cum all over my hand.

Brad was so thankful that he had tears in his eyes as I helped him out of the tub and dried his wet body. While he watched me, I reached under my skirt and removed my drawers, hiding them in a box, and then hugged him tight while I whispered into his ear that I wanted him to have my body. When I heard the others leave to go outside, I lay back on the table and opened my legs for him. It was a bit clumsy but he was able to hobble till he was able to lay on top of me. Because of the circumstances, this would have to be a quickie, so as Brad lay his weight on top of me, I reached between us and guided his, once again, hard cock into my love hole.

Instinctively, Brad began to push and pump and I was very slippery today so it only took a few seconds before he was fully inside me. He was bigger than Robert and William, by quite a bit, and felt way better than Earl had inside me. It may have been that I was more experienced now and was doing this because I wanted to give him pleasure or the fact that he had the longest penis I had ever felt, but either way it felt absolutely wonderful.

Brad began to stroke his cock in and out of my vagina. Since I had given him relief with my hand just minutes before he was able to enjoy being in me for a few minutes before he began to jerk faster and make the sounds that I knew signaled he was about to shoot his sperm inside me. Right then I decided I would let him cum inside me and found myself reaching my first real orgasm. I came hard and kissed him hard to hide both of our moans. I had my legs wrapped tightly around him and felt him pulse several times deep inside me.

Prior to this time, all of my sexual exploration had been directed by my husband, this time I did it because I wanted to and I absolutely loved it. We came down together and kissed while holding each other. We both began to speak at the same time and both said "I Love you" simultaneously. We both blushed and giggled as we sat up, embarrassed by our inappropriate outburst and the passion we had both felt. I would have liked to lay with him forever, letting him have my body as often as he wanted, but the sounds of the others approaching the cabin caused me to quickly make myself presentable and begin dressing Brad. After I had his underpants on, his mother took over dressing him, and I went into the cave to gather my thoughts. A woman just knows when she is pregnant and I knew I was pregnant.

Brad felt asleep within minutes and I hung another blanket to give is mother privacy while she had her bath. We emptied the tub and filled it with fresh hot water. Since we were both women and had seen each other nude when we would bathe in the river, I sat with her and visited while she washed herself. Our cabin had only oil cloth windows but during the light of day it was very light inside. I noticed her breasts and realized that even though I had seen breasts many times, it was always briefly in passing, or like when we would all bathe in the river, we were preoccupied with washing ourselves. Today I was able to sit and carefully look at her, somewhat saggy but attractive, breasts. Those breasts had nursed the man who had, probably, just made me pregnant.

Polly began to unburden herself by telling me that God was punishing her and her husband because she had agreed to let Earl have her body in exchange for passage to the gold fields. I asked her what Earl had done to her but she defended Earl, saying that it was her and her husband's fault.

Apparently, back in St. Louis, Earl had come into the cafe where Polly worked, waiting tables, and had taken a liking to her. Polly had avoided his advances and never mentioned his advances to her husband, but when he announced that he was going to lead a Wagon Train to the California Territory she asked Earl to allow her family to go with them.

Polly said that she would have found a way to meet Earl in private and let him have his fun but Earl acted like he wanted to destroy her marriage. Earl, said she and her family could go but that she had to allow him his pleasure any time he wanted it and that included if her husband was present. Because she wasn't terribly opposed to having sex with Earl, Polly convinced John, her husband, that they should move to the California Territory and get rich picking up the gold that lay everywhere there. She explained that the Wagon Master would not allow a woman to go with them unless she was willing to do as he said, and that included pretending to be his wife some evenings. John hated the idea of sharing his wife but he also was greedy enough to want to be rich. Over a couple weeks of his wife telling him how she would be only doing it for their family he eventually agreed, saying he would go elsewhere when she was with Earl.

I learned that she had been with Earl the time I noticed, but she had also allowed him his pleasure two other times and one was during a heavy rain so John was not able to leave while she opened her legs for this man. In the small wagon had to be within inches of her husband as she let Earl have his way with her. Polly said that Earl seemed to take great pleasure in sexing her in front of her husband. John must have been incredible hurt to see his wife let another man into her body. She told me that is why she did not complain when John went to the bath house in Independence. According to her, he was just evening the score. When she asked me if Earl had gotten his, from me, I truthfully admitted he did, the night he abandoned us. She had learned that Earl had made the same or a similar deal with each of the families that had a woman in their wagon. Apparently, Earl had told her that he wanted me in the worst way. However, Robert and William had convinced him, because of my youth, he needed to allow them time to convince me to do what they had agreed to.

On the one hand I was pissed that my husband and his Father had used me as chattel, just to be allowed to be part of Earl's wagon train. Williams comments about me being an asset, for them, now made more sense. On the other hand, I realized that I had experienced more than most women do in a lifetime. Most women tried to be virgin when they married the first time. If their husband died young or left them, they were then damaged goods and often allowed men liberties in the hopes they would marry them. Otherwise, they remained faithful to just their husband. That was not all women, I believe that nearly half of the women had more than one lover in her lifetime. My mother made it a point to frequently tell me, and my two sisters, that she was a virgin until her wedding night. Here I was married, for only a couple months, and had three men push their penises inside my body and I had touched other men and let other men touch me. None of those experiences, had been particularly bad. Besides, I was pretty sure I had let a man, who was not my husband, get me pregnant.

On an impulse, I asked Polly if she would like for me to wash her back. It was different washing a woman but she kept telling me that it felt heavenly. When I washed her hair, she told me that no one had washed her hair, for her, since she was a little girl. We were very close as I squeezed the last of the rinse water from her hair when she reached up, pulling me close, and kissed me. It was a hurried kiss that landed half on my mouth and half on my cheek. I was stunned but didn't pull away. Polly took this as consent and kissed me again, this time right on my lips. I found myself responding and I kissed her back. This seemed even more taboo than what I had just done with her son as we made out frantically while I reached for and massaged her breasts. Polly had one arm around my neck, holding me tight as we kissed and her other hand was between her legs as she rubbed herself feverishly. Her breasts felt good in my hand and I gentle rolled her nipples between my fingers, just like I like to have mine played with. Unlike Robert, I knew how to touch a woman's breasts. She reached her peak in just a couple minutes and when she had recovered, she whispered that it was better than she ever had with her husband.

14 CHAPTER FOURTEEN

Night came quickly and while William and John found sleeping places in the cave, the rest of us slept in the cabin. Brad tossed and turned most of the night and I woke several times to check on him. He was feverish so I would wipe his brow with a cool damp cloth and then kiss his lips gently while he slept. Robert wanted to have sex since he knew he would be gone for at least ten days and maybe longer. We made a place to sleep on the floor and when Brad and his Mother had fallen asleep, I raised my night gown and let Robert enter me from behind. He whispered that I was really wet and I told him that I wanted him cum inside me that night. This excited him and he came within a minute, filling me with his potent sperm, even if it was already too late for his sperm to do its job.

The next morning, we were all awake before dawn. Polly would be going with Robert to take care of Brad in the back of the wagon. We helped Brad into the lower bunk that I had usually shared with my husband and the men had fashioned a couple belts to secure Brad to prevent him from falling out of the bunk as the wagon bounced across the trail.

Robert took some food and a large bag of the hardtack I had made, with them. He hitched all four of our horses to the wagon, even though it was basically empty, because he planned to fill the wagon with supplies that travelers might need, and purchase, while on the trail. He also planned to bring back a large quantity of grain for the animals. While the animals could graze on plants they found along the trail, especially along streams, that was not enough for an animal that worked hard pulling a wagon every day. A working animal needed the extra energy the grain provided, to stay healthy and not lose weight.

John spent a few minutes with his son, knowing it may be the last time he would see him, and then, with hugs and kisses all around, they left just as it was getting light. William, John and I went back into the cabin and sat quietly drinking coffee while we waited for it to become daylight. When the light was better John moved the horses to better grazing and continued repairing his wagon.

That afternoon John and William went hunting and were able to kill another buffalo. We had built a crude smoke house and the meat from our buffalo was coming along nicely. I had also sliced some of the lean meat and dried it in the warming oven of my stove to make jerky. It required a lot of our salt but the meat would last for months. We processed the animal John had shot and I promised to give him dried and salted meat to take with him on his travels

Evening came too soon and we were all exhausted. I slept in the cabin and the men slept in the cave. Each day was a repeat of the same with me cooking for and helping the men when I could. John's plan was to follow Robert and Polly after resting the animals for three more days but the animals were not recovering as fast as everyone had hoped. On the fourth day William and John came to an agreement that would allow John to travel to meet his wife and son. John would give us the two weakest horses as well as some of the items he had stored in our cave. It was partially payment for what Robert was doing for his son and partially because he had no way to take any more with him. He planned to leave the morning of the fifth day but while Robert expected to make the trip in an empty wagon in 5 days, he would be at least ten days going back to Independence with a fully loaded wagon.

Robert's return trip would also take close to ten days because the wagon would be heavy and Robert was careful not to abuse our horses. Robert would most likely meet John on the trail and report to him, where his wife was staying and how his son was doing.

With plans to leave in the morning, John loaded the meat and a bag of my hardtack with the rest of his supplies. He was anxious to follow his wife but there was an air of nervousness between him and William. Their intentions became clear after they had finished their evening meal. William told me, when John went outside to move his horses to better grass, one more time, that John had paid for a bath and that he had paid two dollars instead of the fifty cents we had advertised. William looked me in the eye and told me to give John what he wanted.

I knew what John would want and I wasn't exactly opposed to letting him have it. He was a good-looking man that in many ways reminded me of my Father. What angered me was that William was selling me and keeping the money. I was once again an asset for William. I told William, in no uncertain terms that I would provide a bath for John, and even, as a courtesy, wash his back but any extras would not happen unless I received all of the money.

William threatened me that I would do as I was told but when I stood my ground, telling him I was not married to him, he backed off. Still, he had not given me the money. I filled a tub of hot water for John and prepared to step out of the curtained area, until he was in the tub. When John suggested I stay, I told him that probably was not a good idea. He told me flat out, that he had paid three dollars for this bath and he expected more than hot water for that price.

William heard our exchange and quickly brought me two dollars. I looked at it and said I wanted it all so he brought the remaining dollar and went back to the cave in a huff telling me that he would have a talk with Robert about this. I intended to have a talk with Robert about this as well.

I turned to John, apologized for my Father-in-law, and began unbuttoning his shirt. It had only been four days since his last bath and with the weather cool John didn't smell too bad as I helped him undress. He had a nice body, for an older man, and more chest hair than I had ever seen. I saw that his son had taken after his dad in the penis department. John was not fully erect, but I could tell already tell, he was going to be large.

While I let John soak in the hot water I stood at the foot of the tub and slowly removed my clothes. I took them all off as I knew they would soon be off anyway. This had the desired effect and his penis was soon poking up above the water. I washed his back as sensuously as I knew how. Rather than stand behind him where it was easiest for me, I stood by his side letting him see and touch my breasts. When I moved to wash his front, he worked his finger into my vagina and fingered me while I stroked his stiff penis. He took a long time before he started panting like he was going to shoot his sperm. Before he came, he pushed my hand away. I knew what he wanted so I helped him out of the tub and dried his body with a towel. When he was dry, he pushed me back on the table and moved between my legs. I was looking forward to what we were about to do and knew I would have my husband's approval when he returned. John was experienced and he used me for several minutes before Cumming inside the vagina his son had filled yesterday. He felt good but looked sad as he put his clean clothes on. I think he felt he had to get even with his wife and hopefully I was the last woman he needed to use before he would be able to forgive his wife.

When he went to bed, I took the money he had given William and hid it in the bottom of the bag I kept my period pads in. I knew a man would never look in there, let alone put his hand in the bag to search for something hidden in the bottom. The next morning John left early but not before hugging me and whispering "Thank you". William and I kept our distance from each other as he were still angry that I had taken the money he had tried to keep for selling my body. I was just fine with that because I was still angry at him for doing it and trying to keep the money. Because of the circumstances I would have let John have my body for free but it angered me that William thought of me as a whore to be sold.

15 CHAPTER FIFTEEN

It had been ten days since Robert left and five days since John had left. William and I had developed a sort of truce. I hoped and thought that John and Robert would be meeting on the trail any time now. I wondered if John would think he had pulled one over on Robert by having sex with his wife or if he would feel badly for what he had done. I hoped he felt badly so that his marriage could begin to heal.

On the eleventh night William came to me and asked if I would fill the bath tub for him and wash his back. I wanted to tell him to do it himself but agreed knowing that Robert would want me to. I filled the tub and didn't bother to put up a blanket for privacy. William stripped off and I noticed he was not even a little bit hard.

As a show of good faith, (Literally) when William had immersed himself in the hot water, I stood at the foot of the tub and began to remove my clothes. I did it slowly and by the time my breasts were bare William was fully hard and sticking up above the water. I was wearing drawers so I saw no point in leaving them on. I turned around, giving William a nice view of my bottom, as I pulled the drawers down and off, to stand naked before him.

When I knelt next to him, he began to apologize but I shushed him by putting a finger on his lips and told him that Robert would want me to do this. He seemed relieved and lay back in the tub with his penis pointing toward the ceiling. I pushed his body forward and began washing his back. When I moved to his front, I first washed him but then dropped all pretense of doing anything but trying to make him cum for me. I knelt beside the tub where William could see me while I stroked his cock. This time I did not wait for him to grab my breast, I used my free hand to take is left hand and place it on my breast.

William must have masturbated earlier in the day because, even though he was hard, he was not reaching his climax. It seems funny now but even though I was allowing him to fondle my breasts, I decided to let him do more because my arm was getting tired. Not because I wanted it, but because I wanted him to finish. I leaned closer to him and whispered, even though we were alone and no one would have heard me even if I had screamed, "When you cum I want you to stick your finger in my cunt". That was his word for it, not mine, and it had the desired effect. He shot cum all over my arm and shoulder.

I kept my word and walked, on my knees, a step closer so he could easily push his finger into me. I gentle stroked his now softening penis for a few minutes while he fingered me. I wasn't even close to getting my climax but it felt good to have something inside me after almost a week. I mentally chastised myself for thinking that way but had to admit I was enjoying his finger.

We both went to bed feeling better and I used my fingers to make myself shudder. I thought of all the things I had done with Brad, John, and William, reaching a very nice release. The next day both William and I seemed happier and at lunch, our mid-day meal, William commented on how much he enjoyed what we had done. Somehow, in the bright light of day, it embarrassed me and I blushed as I thanked him.

Of course, William had an ulterior motive and at supper he asked me if we could do it again tonight. I should have just refused but I thought I was being practical when I told him that I was not going to fill and drain the bath tub two nights in a row. William had a practical answer, he would just remove his pants and we could play on the table I used for my bed. Just like with his son, I was not going to let myself be laying down with him because I knew I could easily lose control of the situation.

I knew, deep down, that it was probably only a matter of time before William would know what I felt like inside. Up until now, Robert had agreed that no one should put his penis inside me so they didn't accidently get me pregnant. If I didn't start my period in four or five days, and was pregnant, that barrier would be removed, at least for nine months and I suspected that Robert would want to see me open my legs for another man. Since his Poppa was the only other man for what might be a hundred miles, I knew Robert would be asking me to let his Poppa into my body.

I told William that I would not let him into my bed but I would help him masturbate before he went to sleep. He tried suggesting that he hoped we could do more than masturbate, telling me it had been over a year since he had been with a woman. He claimed, his last woman had been paid so she made sure it was over quickly. I told him that it was not going to happen without Robert's approval and that I knew his son would not want me to do it until I was pregnant. I told him I would come to the cave when he went to bed and help him achieve relief.

I wanted to give William easy access, because I did enjoy feeling his fingers inside me, so when William went to the cave to sleep, I stripped off my clothes and covered myself with a warm quilt. The cave where William slept was a little cool, as compared to the cabin, where the stove burned constantly. The cave was probably much better for sleeping but not so good for playing.

By the time I had joined William he had stripped naked and was under the covers. He raised the covers and invited me to join him. I knew better than to allow that because he would want and have full sex if I lay with him. Instead, I had him sit up next to me and pulled the covers over the both of us. I told him that this time he had to make me feel good while I would make him feel good. He tried to say he needed to use his cock for that but easily gave in and began to play with me. We leaned against each other and slowly played with each other's private parts.

He was very good as he pushed first one then two fingers inside me while rubbing the pad of his thumb over my clit. It didn't take long before I reached a powerful climax. Not as good as the one Brad had given me but very good. William let me recover for a few minutes and I turned to take care of him. Since I was sitting next to him, I would sometimes brush my breast against him. In just a minute he shot his sperm all over my chest.

We had given each other powerful climaxes in just a few minutes and as much as I enjoyed it, I knew we could not continue to do this every night or I would end up with his cock inside me. I fell asleep thinking about how I could regulate our sexual play. The problem solved itself around mid-day the next day.

When we heard the call "Hello the house" it startled me but William quickly produced a hand gun and told me to stay back while he found out who was there. It was Jacob, the boy with the birthmark, and his Father, Paul.

Paul was very ill and they could no longer keep up with the others so they were forced to turn back. When they saw our sign, in the same green paint as our wagon, advertising hot baths, they came hoping they could find a place for Paul to recover. After learning that it was us, they came inside and join us for the mid-day meal.

Paul was suffering from a bad cold and probably pneumonia and the flu. I immediately put a kettle of mint tea on the stove and prepared a tincture of Mallow and Stinging Nettles. These were all things I gathered along the trail and had saved them for when they would be needed. Paul had been in the cold dry air for days but now he sat near the warm stove sipping his tea and inhaling the steam from the Mallow and Nettles concoction I had prepared. He soon was coughing up the flem and his sinuses began to run. It took several hours before he was able to relax but was sleeping near the fire before dark.

The first night Jacob slept in the cave with William as Paul continued to sleep in the warm and humid cabin. The second day Jacob and I hauled water to the cabin with buckets. Because he was interested in what I had made the tea from, that had helped his Father so quickly, we took a walk along the creek as I pointed out various plants and other things that could be used as medicine. I am not sure where I had learned it, probably from years of my mother pointing things out when we would go visit friends or by her making a tincture or tea when one of us girls or my Father had an ailment. We sat on a large rock and talked.

Jacob apologized, again, for what he had done. I told him that I understood why he had done it and that he was forgiven. His birth mark really bothered him and he told me that even though he was over twenty years old, he had never even kissed a girl, let alone been with one for sex. He shamefully admitted to me that he went to a whore house in St. Louis but was turned away because none of the girls wanted to touch him. I repeated to him that in time he would find a woman who loved him for who he was. Again, I am sure neither one of us believed me, so to prove my point I pulled him close and kissed his cheek.

Jacob held me tight. It was not a sexual thing but he held me close and this time I kissed him on the lips. I did not see it as cheating on Robert but rather comforting Jacob. I slowly pulled back from his arms, not wanting this to get out of hand after probably getting myself with child when I comforted Brad. We walked back to the cabin like close friends.

My period should have been upon me but I was not feeling any of the signs, I was not irritable nor was my tummy upset. In fact, I felt wonderful. I knew Robert would be home very soon so I planned what I would tell him.

That evening Jacob asked what they owed for our hospitality, the meals, and for nursing his Father. William started to tally what they owed until I looked at him and told him that there would be no charge. Jacob was relieved saying that they had very little money but that they would pay their due and if there was money left over, he wanted to pay for a bath for his father and for himself.

William wisely did not challenge my decision, so I advised Jacob that for the price of one dollar I would allow them each a hot bath. That was still a great deal of money, even though John had paid three dollars but I was not planning on providing as much as I had provided for John. Paul decided that he was feeling well enough to sleep in the cave so that I could have my bed back.

I put a blanket up around the tub for privacy and to keep it even warmer for the person bathing. Paul went first and when he was embarrassed to remove his underpants I turned away and let him make his way into the tub. I gave him the usual washing of his back and washing his hair. After he had finished washing himself, I helped him out of the tub. His manhood was getting pretty stiff but he had the courtesy to turn away. I marveled at how much my life had changed in the past few months.

Jacob started to get into the tub of dirty water before I stopped him. If they paid for a hot bath, I would give them clean and hot water. I drained and cleaned the tub before filling it with hot water. I then shooed the rest of them out into the cave and begin undressing Jacob. I held a finger to his lips when he began to speak and whispered to him that I wanted to do this. I took each piece of his clothing off, except his underpants, and then removed my dress and camisole leaving me topless and only wearing the panties from my wedding set.

I put my arms around his neck and, pulled him close, kissing him firmly on the lips. our bodies touched and my bare breasts rubbed against his chest. I soon felt his hardness poking my lower belly so I knelt down and removed his underpants. His penis was very nice, bigger than Robert but not as big as Brad or John. I gave it a couple gentle strokes and told him to get in the tub. He got the usual back wash and I washed his hair. I knelt down next to the tub and rubbed his penis with my left hand while letting him rub my breasts with his left hand. It only took a minute for him to shoot his sperm all over my hand.

After he joined the others in the cave, I washed their clothes and hung them behind the stove to dry. The hot stove would easily dry them before morning. I placed the dollar I had been given in my hiding place and went to bed. Remembering how Jacob had kissed me and how his penis felt in my hand had me touching myself between my legs and I too had a strong cum. Now that I knew what a strong climax felt like, it was easier to make them happen. The next morning, we all slept later than usual.

Paul was better but still not ready to travel. Their horses, like the rest of the travelers, needed more time to recover, so they helped around the camp and Jacob worked on their wagon to waterproof it and make it ready to travel. That afternoon Jacob brought a stack of beaver pelts in to me. He gave me four of them as extra payment for his bath. I knew that they had little money, so I purchased eight more for three dollars cash. I hoped they would be worth much more than what I had paid for them, in Independence. It turned out that Jacob was a crack shot and his Father was a good trapper, so they had harvested a few animals each night when they camped along the river.

Robert came home the next day with our wagon full of things he had bought in Independence. There were large bags of flour, salt, sugar, cornmeal and many other things for the kitchen. There were also many bags of oats for the horses. There were several cases of whiskey, Brandy, and wine. The sad news was that Brad did not make it and he had died just before they reached Independence. Robert had buried him on a bluff overlooking the Missouri river and his Mother, Polly had ridden with Robert into Independence and then back toward our cabin until they met John on the trail.

John and Polly decided to winter near the city and planned to leave for the California gold fields as early as possible in the Spring.

Robert backed the wagon up against the cabin and we, again, had our home complete. He was anxious to have sex, after being away for over two weeks. I let Robert believe that I was anxious too but, inside, I was really more concerned with how my husband would react to all the news I had to tell him. When Robert took his bath, I could tell that Jacob was a little upset. He had a crush on me and now had to accept the reality that I was married to Robert.

Everyone went to bed early because it got dark early and candles and lamp oil were precious. Robert wanted this because we would have several hours to become reacquainted. Even though we had only been married a few months I knew Robert would be most agreeable if I was naked and he was hard. I remade our bed in the wagon, which afforded us more privacy, and I got naked for my husband. When we were under the covers, I whispered that a lot has happened since he left.

Robert thought he knew what had happened and asked if his Father has wanted me to masturbate him again. I honestly told him yes, but that wasn't the big news. I reminded him that I had let him cum inside me just before he went away. I told him that I should have had my visitor by now so I suspected that I was with child. He was elated, kissing me repeatedly, telling me that he loved me and that I would be a great Mother. When he had calmed down, I asked him if he enjoyed seeing when I touched his Father. He said "You know I did." I teased my horny husband, saying that William made me do it for another guy while he was gone. Robert immediately named John, Paul and Jacob, wanting to know all the details. I refused to tell him exactly who I did it for, but explained that William had told the other man that he could have full sex with me for three dollars.

Robert predictably thought it was Jacob, saying he thought Jacob was the only one young and dumb enough to pay three dollars to have sex with me. I didn't say anything but suddenly didn't feel quite as bad, as I had, for lying to him about who got me pregnant. I told him the story of how William tried to keep the money and how he had lied about how much he had received. When I told him how I had collected the entire amount he laughed but wanted to know all the details. I told him how John had done me on the table after his bath. I explained that I felt he was getting even with his wife for having sex with Earl. I sugar coated it by telling him that, at the time, I did not know I was pregnant, so I made him pull out. I told him John had shot his baby batter over my bare breasts, when in fact, he had shot every drop deep inside me.

Robert did not wait to hear more and mounted me. He was over excited, so he only lasted for a few strokes. At least now that I was pregnant, he was able to shoot inside me. I let him know that I had given Jacob hand relief with his bath and told him that I had received a beaver pelt for my efforts. Again, this was not exactly true but it didn't seem to matter. He mounted me again and this time I had a little climax. I know he would have like to hear what Polly and I had done and I know he would have risen to the occasion again, if I told him, but I decided to keep that just for me.

16 CHAPTER SIXTEEN

After another day and some grain for the horses Paul and Jacob were ready to move on. They decided to hunt and trap their way North and West. Robert explained to Paul and Jacob that, our friend, John had given him the remains of the wagon they had lost and any of the contents that might still be useable. They agreed to travel with Robert and help him find and load the materials into our wagon before continuing on their way. Robert again moved the wagon from the side of the cabin and they left the next morning. Jacob made a point of coming back into the cabin and kissing me before they left.

I was suddenly left alone with William again. He wanted full sex but I was not prepared to give him what he wanted. I told him that it was a good night for a bath and then explained that he could give me my bath first. At first, he acted like I had insulted him but when he understood that it was my way or no way he agreed and he filled the tub. I gave him some of what he wanted by removing my clothes in front of him and sat back to enjoy a hot bath. He washed my back and I did my own hair while he watched my breasts jiggle as I worked my fingers through the hair. When I was done, I lay back and told him to do my front. I closed my eyes and enjoyed a half hour of William ministering to my coochie, cunt as he called it, and was feeling mellow when the water was cool and he was done.

When I had refilled the tub, I had William strip and I preformed the requisite back and hair washing for him. I decided that honesty was the best policy, so I told him that I had enjoyed our last time together, probably too much, but that I did not want to have full on sex with him unless Robert knew in advance. I told him that Robert was aware the first time I was completely nude while I washed him and assured William that his son would probably want me to allow him even more. Robert had spilled the beans, about me being pregnant, the next morning to everyone so William reasoned that no harm would be done if he was allowed inside my body. I compromised saying he could shoot his sperm on me but not in me. With that he pushed me back on the table and stood between my legs. He bent my legs back and apart causing my womanhood to open like a flower. If he chose to force me now, I probably could not stop him. I was in a dangerous position, literally, but the thrill of being so exposed, in front of my husband's Father, felt wonderful. I taunted him as he masturbated only inches from my hole, telling him that soon I would let him put his cock in me. With that, he shot several hot streams of his sperm right on my open hole and all over the hair that surrounded it. If I had not been pregnant, I would have been worried about his juice entering me but now I just smiled and used my finger to force some of his sperm inside my coochie.

Robert returned a few days later with everything John and Polly had left after the accident, including the disassembled wagon all piled into our wagon. He spent several days repairing and rebuilding the broken wagon, using the few tools he had brought along, until it was as good as new. He even gave it a coat of green paint. Our guests did not come often but with winter in full swing it was understandable. It seemed that every week or so a wagon with two or three half frozen men would stop. They were predictably the ones who had gold fever so bad that they would risk their lives to get an early start on their trip to the gold fields.

The first such wagon pulled in during a winter snow storm with so much snow blowing about it created blizzard conditions. I was surprised that they were even able to find us. The men were half frozen and I later learned that the horses had found the way without help from their owners. They looked like two brothers but I later learned they were cousins, and I welcomed them into our home. Robert put their team in the shelter, he had built for our horses, giving them all much needed grain to help fend off the cold.
``

After both men were sufficiently thawed in front of the stove, we ate a hearty meal. The men had shed their layers of clothing and were quite handsome. I wondered if they would want extra services with their bath and part of me hoped they did but this was the first time Robert was home when it happened. Well not counting Brad, actually this was the first time Robert was home and knew what I would be doing. They had come all the way from St. Louis and brought news that the Cholera epidemic was still going strong. One thought he knew of my friend Emily and reported that he thought she had married a man old enough to be her Father or Grandfather.

Robert did not seem as anxious, as he was normally, for me to do something that would excite him sexually. After we had all eaten and the men were playing a friendly game of cards, I pulled Robert into the wagon and whispered into his ear that if he wanted me to do anything with these men, he would have to arrange it. I had learned to be careful around Robert, knowing how much it turned him on to share me, so I cautioned him that I would only be with one man at a time. Robert suggested that I offer to do more when I helped them with their baths and I reminded him that I was not a whore.

I smiled inside because Robert could not find a the courage to tell the men that I was available. He had made it clear that he wanted me to do something, when we talked, but this time added that I did not have to open my legs for them. if I didn't want to. Maybe he felt insecure because they were so good looking. When they took a break from the game and went outside to smoke, Robert pulled his Father aside and whispered to him. They were still discussing it when the others came back in, saying it was getting colder outside.

William brought out a bottle of the whiskey Robert had brought back from Independence and after a few shots were consumed, he asked the men if they were going to partake in a hot bath. When they responded that they would, I busied myself with filling the water barrel with buckets of water I carried from the creek. On one trip I heard William say that the hot bath was fifty cents and anything else was between them and me. William looked directly at me when the younger, and best looking one, suggested that I did not look like the type of girl that was for sale. William chuckled and told him that I was my own woman and he might be surprised by me.

William may have found a way to keep from having to put a price on my services but I could just as easily not provide any extra services. the dollar we would make from the bath was good money and it would serve Robert and his Father right. I announced to the group that we would start the baths after the evening meal and told them that the rest of them would have to either go outside or into the cave while I helped the first one bathe. I had them all, including Robert and William, strip down to their long-handled underwear and washed all their clothes. The stove was so hot that by hanging them behind the stove, it would only take a short time for the clothes to dry.

Comment [A]: e

Who went first was decided by the toss of a coin and the second-best looking guest won the opportunity to go first. He may have been the second best looking but he was still a very handsome guy. He was a little full of himself and began trying to grab me as soon as he had sat down into the hot water. I was playful and told him that I would wash his back and hair as part of the deal but if he grabbed me again it was going to cost him double. He didn't even flinch as he grabbed my breast through my dress and said that was fine with him. He had paid Robert and William his fifty cents before we started and when I held my hand out, he offered that there was an additional dollar in the pocket of his undershirt. I collected it and since he was paying triple, I decided to let him have some fun. I stood at the foot of the tub and slowly removed my dress, leaving just left my panties on. My boobs took a good workout as he felt me up and down while I helped him wash. When I began to masturbate him, he placed his hand on my bottom and asked "How much for this." I assured him he did not have enough money and he accepted that while I stroked him to completion. After drying him, and letting him put on his outer clothes, I sent him to the cave with the others. I kept his underwear to wash later.

The extra dollar was quickly put in my hiding place. I dressed and I prepared a hot bath for the next man, who I had learned earlier, was his cousin. This man was shy and a bit timid but there was something about him that I found very attractive. I was looking forward to providing extras for him. He blushed and asked me to turn away as he removed his clothes and climbed into the tub. I knew he would be too shy to try anything, so without asking, I removed my dress and began washing his back. I teased that it was so that I did not get the dress wet but the real reason was to make myself available to this young man.

When his back and hair were clean, I sat beside him and we talked. I thanked him for the complement earlier, when he said I was not a whore, and he told me that he didn't think I was but his cousin had insisted that he bring a dollar in with him for any extras I might provide. I whispered that I had let his cousin see my breasts and gave him a little help with my hand to earn his dollar. He looked down and said that he guessed I had earned his dollar as well. I whispered that if he promised not to tell anyone he might have a bit more fun than his cousin had. He like this idea and eagerly agreed. I leaned in to him and kissed him while I stroked his thick cock. I wanted to make him feel good but the kissing was making it good for me as much as it was for him. After he had his release, I helped him dry and then whispered not to make any noise.

I sat back against the bench we had used for a table and removed my panties. We kissed for a while and then I lay back with my legs open, offering myself to him. He did not disappoint and was soon thrusting between my legs. I kind of lost track of time and the next thing I knew he was Cumming inside me. I again made sure he would keep what happened a secret, and let him dress to join the others.

Before we parted, he gave me his dollar. Because I wanted to be with him, I had not collected before we played but he was honest and gave me the dollar saying he wished he had more to give.

The young men stayed one more day, to recover and let their horses rest, but the next morning they were on their way to find the gold that was to be had in California. The days were short and the nights were long so with little to do we all hunkered down for the winter. Now Robert liked the long nights because we would go to the wagon, or on really cold nights make a bed by the stove in the cabin, and the sex was wonderful. Robert was becoming more comfortable with my body and lasted a little longer. We no longer had to worry about pregnancy so we were able to enjoy each other. Sometimes we would wake up in the middle of the night and have sex. It was one of those late-night sessions that Robert chose to redeem my wedding night promise.

Robert had been building up to asking me for several days by asking if I remembered my promise and asking what might be acceptable. I used this opportunity to tell him that it had to be something just for him and then added that it could not be painful. He seemed ok with this so I began to wonder what he had in mind. A couple nights later, in the wee hours of the morning, he gently woke me by kissing my neck and whispered his request.

My husband wanted me to let him have sex with me and then to put his penis in my mouth. He then wanted me to suck him till he was hard again. He wanted me to keep doing it until he could not get hard again. Now you will remember that I had considered doing parts of this from the beginning. I had envisioned that I would do it right after he had his bath, not in the middle of the night after working all day and having sex the night before

But a promise is a promise so I would try to ignore any off putting smell or taste. I pulled my husband on top of me while I whispered back to him that I would suck him as much as he wanted. This made him shoot quick, like when we were first married. When I felt him start to slip out of my coochie, I snuggled down under the covers and took him in my mouth. At first, I did not think I could do it. The smell was awful and he tasted bad too. There was his body odor and a strong womanly smell that could have only come from between my legs. He tasted like my coochie and of pee too. I knew that from now on I would only do this after he had his bath.

I didn't know how hard to suck but Robert must have loved it because he was moaning so loud. I enjoyed the power it gave me over my husband but was also afraid his father would hear us in the cave. It didn't take long before my husband was hard, again. I asked him how he wanted me and he said, "From behind," so I got on my knees and leaned forward with my bottom up in the air. This time, Robert lasted longer before shooting a second load of baby juice into me. The position had me on the verge of a climax when he came. I playfully complained that I was almost there and he told me that tonight it was only about him, but maybe I would get mine on the next try.

I slipped back under the covers and began sucking him again. This time there was a fresh coating of his sperm and my juices but for some reason they did not seem as bad. Maybe I was just used to it now. I licked the juice from his penis like it was a lolly pop and took him in my mouth. This time it took him longer to rise to the occasion. I found myself wondering if Polly would have tasted like this if we had the opportunity to go further than we did the night she took her bath. My husband was hard and beginning to pant, but he put his hands on my head and would not let me up. He whispered that it felt fantastic, and begged me to keep going. A couple times he pushed too far and it caused me to gag but I continued to suck him until he shot his sperm into my mouth.

When he released me, I kissed my way up his chest, so he would not suspect anything, and when I got to his lips, I kissed him hard and used my tongue to push his sperm into his mouth. Of course, he spit, gagged, and cussed as he rolled away from me, angerly asking why I had done it. I told him what is good for the goose is good for the gander. When he returned to our bed, after drinking water and a shot of whiskey, I kissed him again and he returned the kiss telling me my mouth smelled like my coochie. He also shyly admitted that he kind of liked it. I wet a finger, between my legs, and offered it to him. He was sucking my finger, like a baby on a tit, when he fell asleep.

17 CHAPTER SEVENTEEN

During next few days a tension started to build. Robert would suggest to me that I let his Poppa enjoy my body and I would tell him that he had to arrange it with his Father if he wanted me to do that. William would playfully grab my breasts and tell me that he wanted me, when Robert would step out to feed the horses. I would tell him he had to ask his Son. Rather than talk about it, both men kept to themselves and refused to start a conversation. I understood because I could not imagine asking my Mother to let me have sex with my Father, but at first, I enjoyed watching them squirm. After a couple days I tired of them not talking and brought the subject up that night at the evening meal.

I had made a stew with lots of meat, potatoes and vegetables. We also had fresh bread. Everyone was enjoying the feast when I said to Robert, "So, do you want me to sleep with your Poppa tonight? Both Robert and his Poppa nearly choked on their food. Before he could answer, I continued. I know you have been wanting me to sleep with him, and your Poppa has been wanting me, so can I do it tonight? My husband was blushing, bright red, and looking at his plate. William was not doing much better. When my husband stuttered that he did not care, it kind of upset me, so I told him that this time he could not watch. I told my husband that I wanted to spend the night in William's bed and return to him after we were done.

Things were pretty quiet after that and the men would not look at each other. I didn't want this to go bad so I retrieved a bottle of the whiskey from the cave and poured three cups. I gave one to each of the men and kept one for myself. It burned much more than I remembered so I added a bit of water to mine. A second round had lifted the mood considerably. By time we finished the bottle we were all laughing and I was teasing the men.

I teased William that he had been wanting me for a long time and that soon he would have his chance. William said that of course he wanted me because I was young and beautiful. That made me feel good and I teased my husband that I was going to be the best his Father ever had. Robert teased right back, asking who was going to make him feel good.

The whiskey made me feel wobbly as I put things away and prepared for bed. To help protect my husband's pride, I whispered into his ear that I would come to his bed with his Poppa's sperm in my kitty and that I wanted him to have sex with me to push it even deeper into my womb. After our meal, I suggested William go to the cave while I put up a blanket over the entrance to the cave. I know Robert was a bit disappointed but I whispered to him that he could still hear everything but that tonight I wanted privacy. I don't think my husband anticipated that I would want to enjoy my time with his Poppa.

I stood kissing my husband for several minutes and then went to the cave knowing that this would probably become a regular event from now on. William had left a small candle burning so I stood near his bed and undressed. I could have left my clothes on and let William remove them a piece at a time but we all knew where this would end so I made it easier for both of us. When I was naked, I stood near the bed and let William look at my body. This time when he raised the blankets, I slipped in beside him, knowing what was about to happen. William also knew where this would end and he was naked under the blanket.

I was not in love with William but we had been together for several months. He had seen my body, or parts of my body, numerous times. I wanted his approval, I wanted my husband's approval, and making love to my husband's Father appealed to me for some reason. Maybe it was a twisted way for me to make this man, who seemed to consider me as a servant and chattel, desire me and work hard to try and please me.

I did not mis-speak above, I did not plan to just let William use my vagina as a warm receptacle for his sperm. I was going to be the best piece of ass he ever had and I planned to enjoy doing it. I snuggled under the covers, letting my body rub against William. As I kissed down his chest his hands were everywhere. I let him touch where he wanted and he didn't waste time with the less important areas. He had two fingers of one hand in my vagina while his other hand played with my back side. No one had ever touched me there and it added to the taboo nature of what we were doing. I kissed him hard, sucking his tongue into my mouth while he pushed his penis against my belly. In seconds we were both so excited that there was no seduction just raw lust as we rushed to complete the act.

A second later he was on top of me, forcing my legs apart and pushing his penis into me. My plan to tease him for a long time before letting him have my body went out the window and I reached between us to guide his cock into my body. As William would say, I guided his cock into my cunt, and I was loving it. He only lasted a few minutes, driving himself into me, before he stopped and tensed. I could feel his cock jerking and felt his sperm being injected deep inside me.

I cuddled with him for a while with my head on his chest. The sex, we just had, was animalistic and felt wonderful but I wanted more so I began to slowly stroke his cock. He was getting stiffer but was still not hard enough to give me pleasure, so I began whispering in his ear. I asked him if he liked what we just did. I told him that I liked it when he put his finger in my bottom. I told him that I was looking forward to spreading my legs for him and he was hard again.

This time William mounted me and slowly pumped into me. I was able to lay back and enjoy the feeling. William kissed me and then kissed my neck. I always like having my neck kissed but tonight it felt fantastic. I was wet and the sperm he had pumped into me earlier was leaking out creating a huge wet spot on the sheet below me. I had a very nice cum and when I told William that I loved his cock, he came inside me again. I let him lay on top of me, as we rested and caught our breath, when he began to doze, I slipped out from under him, collected my clothes and blew out the candle.

There was no reason to put my clothes on so I let William continue to sleep in the wet spot of the bed and went to find my husband. When I slipped under the covers with Robert, I felt several wet spots on the top quilt, where he must have masturbated to completion while waiting for me to return from his Father's bed. It kind of upset me that he used his hand rather than waiting to give me his attention. After all, as far as he knew, I was having sex with his Poppa as a favor to my husband. I am sure he thought I had not enjoyed it near as much as I had.

Robert was particularly amorous and wasted no time pushing his stiff penis into my body to mix his sperm with the two loads his Poppa had left inside me. I had a nice climax with William so I would have been happy to go to sleep but Robert wanted to go again and was not getting stiff. Since dirty talk had worked so well with his Poppa, I did the same for my husband. I began whispering into his ear telling him what his Father had done to me. I embellished a little, but not much, when I told him how good it felt when William was inside me. That did the trick, He mounted me again and we had good reclaiming sex. I had another good climax as my husband finished inside me and we drifted off to sleep with me sleeping in the wet spot this time.

The next day wasn't as awkward as I had feared it would be. But Robert noticcd and pointed out that William had given me a large hickey on my neck. Of course, I was terribly embarrassed but I hugged my husband and turned to present the other side of my neck, telling him he could mark the other side of me. Robert gave my neck a quick suck and left his mark but Williams side was larger and darker. The men seemed fine and were anxious to get more firewood cut in case we received a lot of snow. They did not seem hungover but I was feeling the effects of last night's whiskey. After the mid-day meal, the men went outside and I took a quick nap to help me recover but not before I gave myself a nice cum with my fingers while I thought of what I had done the night before.

That evening I made a nice meal for my two men and I seemed to be the only one who was nervous about what might happen later when we went to bed. Rather than let me stew, William noticed that I was nervous and answered the obvious question for me. Robert and his Poppa had a long talk while they were taking a break from cutting wood. They decided that William would be able to have me whenever he needed me but that would usually be on bath nights because William felt that was about all he could handle. They had also decided that when Robert was gone, William and I would decide where I would sleep while he was gone. Robert did not care if I took care of William's needs more often. It would have been nice if they had asked my opinion, but I was ok with what they had decided. I was going to be letting two men inside me on a regular basis now.

Again, we settled into a comfortable pattern. Bath night happened a couple nights later and this time I was able to tease William for well over an hour before I let him cum. When I returned to his son's bed, I repeated the tease and Robert loved it, teasing me back, that he was glad I was learning new things from his Father. William wanted relief a couple days after that, when Robert had gone hunting, and this time, I felt no guilt as I bent over the table in the cabin and let William use me from behind. It was kind of exciting to hug my husband when he returned, from his hunt, knowing I had another man's sperm inside me.

The one time that I did not like our arraignment, whereby we offered hot baths and other services to people who traveled the trail, was when the old trapper visited. The old man arrived one afternoon and hailed the house. He looked really old and had a mule that was so loaded down with his gear and furs that you could hardly see the mule. After the usual hellos we invited him in and I began to prepare a meal for him. The first thing I noticed was the horrible smell. The old man was certainly a candidate for a bath. We offered him a bath and he claimed that he didn't have any money but William began to make a deal to receive some of the furs in return for a hot bath. The old man wanted more for the furs than they were worth but the smell was making me sick. Maybe it was because I was pregnant and already feeling a tinge of morning sickness. William finally made the deal by explaining that I would wash his back for him. The old man wanted me to join him in the bath. When I refused, he said the deal was off, making it clear that if he wasn't allowed to breed me then the deal was off.

After a long negotiation a deal was struck. We would get most of the furs at a good discount and the old trapper would get me. I didn't like the second part but everyone agreed that it would happen after he was completely washed, I would wash him with my breasts bare. When he was done, I would let him do me from behind, one time. I felt that at least that way I would not have to look at him while he got his relief. When the tub was filled, the men made ready to leave but something about this guy bothered me and I asked them to stay. William seemed a little uncomfortable but Robert acted like I had given him a present. Robert was hard as soon as I removed my dress and stayed that way during the entire bath. I even used the scissors to trim the trapper's fingernails and toe nails. After receiving a very good bath and washing his clothes, the old man looked and smelled much better. He still looked old, old enough to be my grandfather. The loads of grey hairs on his chest were interesting to me but the trapper quickly put his shirt on, leaving his trousers off, so he could have sex with me.

Despite my efforts, his penis was still soft when I dried him off and after I had removed my drawers and knelt in front of him to stroke him, he was still only half hard. I didn't want to put him in my mouth but when my arm began to tire, I knew that was my only hope to get him off. After listening to the negotiations setting this up, I knew the trapper would not honor the deal if he did not have an orgasm. I acted as sexy as possible as I took his limber penis into my mouth. I could see Robert and William in my peripheral vision and they were both discretely rubbing themselves through their trousers. As soon as I knew he was hard, I turned around and presented my bottom to him. I had his attention now and he gave me a good long screwing before he shot inside me. Robert and William let him dress and eat with us before sending him on his way. While they were negotiating and during the meal, the old man had imparted his knowledge of the trails and methods of finding water in the worst desert. He told of areas to the North that would challenge travelers because it appeared that there was no water when it was only a few feet below the surface in places.

The fact was that we made good money. However, it did not make letting him use my vagina, for his pleasure, any more pleasurable for me. What made it worse was that watching me service the trapper made both men were horny. Both men wanted me to use my mouth to please them, like I had with the trapper. At first, I thought they wanted to do it with all of us in the same room, but they opted for privacy. For once I caught a break.

For a couple more weeks, Robert and William shared me as my breasts began to swell and my tummy did too. The days were beginning to get longer and we had more and more warm days. We had discussed when we should leave many times but had conflicting feelings about leaving our winter home. The visitors to our cabin continued to arrive about once a week. There would be one to three guys and depending on what they wanted and what I thought about them, I did everything from just providing hot bath water to, at least for a couple of them, to spreading my legs and enjoying them as much as they enjoyed me.

18 CHAPTER EIGHTEEN

One day we heard a familiar "Hello the house", it was John and Polly. John had found work with a small lumber mill and since he had a strong team, he spent a couple months skidding logs from the forest to the sawmill. The best part of seeing our friends, was that John and Polly were now very much in love and getting along famously. There were hugs all around and we were all anxious to know what they had been doing. We learned that they had been allowed to use a small one room cabin, near the mill, until the work ran out. Even though it was still too early to start towards California, they decided to return to our cabin.

When Polly and I were alone she filled me in on what had happened in her life. Over time John had totally forgiven Polly for her encounters with Earl and he realized that the thought of his wife enjoying another man excited him. Maybe it was the thought of another man enjoying his wife that excited him. Polly also realized that their marriage was more than a contract for sex and now knew that she enjoyed being with other men. After many nights of pillow talk John admitted to Polly that he had sex with me to even the score and Polly sheepishly admitted to John that she and I had played around while she was taking her bath. They both agreed that it was pleasurable, but they only wanted each other. With their secrets out in the open they began to talk about how they could continue to enhance their marriage.

Polly also explained to me that her marriage to John had been arraigned by their parents. They were not forced to marry but it was strongly suggested. Polly and John dated a few times and decided that they would do their parents' will. Being young, John was not too picky about who he had sex with and Polly tried to be a good wife even though she had her eye on another young lad before she was told to marry John. They had made the marriage work and grown to love each other but they had never been in love with each other. She thought that may have been why she had succumbed to Earl's advances.

Polly explained that they had become friends with their neighbors who stayed in the other one room cabin, right next to the cabin John and Polly used. Because they were close, they spent a lot of time together, sharing meals and playing cards. Their neighbors were of similar age and there seemed to be a mutual attraction. Polly admired Ray. The husband's height and strength and John seemed enamored with Susan's, the wife's, large breasts. Likewise, Ray liked Polly's smaller and tighter body while Susan was impressed with Johns gentle demeanor.

It was Polly who broached the subject to Susan one day as they visited while the men were at work. She began by telling her friend about the affair she had with Earl. After she had the other woman wishing that she was the one who had the affair, Polly told her that not only had John forgiven her, he had accepted the idea that she would have sex with other men, and that he now treated her much better than he had treated her before the affair. She left out that her affair had almost destroyed their marriage, and that there were several months of upheaval before they got to the point they were at now.

With Susan's interest, they conspired to fool around with each other's husband, that weekend when they got together to eat and play cards. Of course, they did their best to make it look like their husband's idea. After a great meal the two couples sat down to play cards but this time when the men playfully suggested strip poker, the women reluctantly agreed. They kept the option to stop at any time but privately they had decided that they would at least kiss the other husband and neither woman was planning to make it a chaste kiss,

Both women had to intentionally lose a couple extra hands to lose their clothes soon enough that the husbands would suggest the women start doing other dares if they lost a hand. Because what they were doing was so taboo, they covered the window with a blanket and put the bolt on the door. Susan was especially excited; in the twenty years she had been married to Ray she did not remember a single time that she had sat naked in front of her husband. Tonight, she was sitting naked in front of her husband and in front of another man that she found attractive. John and Polly were also enjoying the game but they were thinking ahead, to having sex with the other couple.

After everyone had lost their clothes, the women made sure they each folded a very good hand, to make it look like they both lost the hand. They let the men believe they reluctantly were agreeing to kiss the other man for two minutes. With the men, also nude, hard and sitting on a straight-backed chair, they straddled the other's husband and wrapped their arms around them. This put their breasts and vaginas against the man who thought he had talked the women into this. At the end of two minutes all four friends were making out and touching the other's sexy parts. It was easy for the men to agree that Polly would stay in her home with Ray, for the night and that Susan would spend the night in her cabin with John. Everyone agreed that they would meet at Ray and Susan's cabin, for breakfast, before sunrise so no one would suspect what they had been up to.

Polly said that they did this every Saturday night for three weeks and that Ray screwed her till she was sore the next morning. Polly told me that during the week John was so amorous that they had sex almost every night. Of course, I told her about some of the men I had been with, but she seemed most interested in my experiences with William. When I told her that he made me feel very good in bed, she asked for details. She asked me later, that same day, if I thought the guys would be interested in a swap.

Of course, I was anxious to swap because I had enjoyed my time with John the last time. This time would be even better because I would not feel guilty for playing with Polly's husband, behind her back, and John would no longer be confused about what he was doing The thing that bothered me, just a little, was the fact that Robert was going to experience Polly while I enjoyed her husband. There was also the matter of what William was going to do while the rest of us played. He had become a part of our sex life, at least for me, and I cared about what he thought and felt. When the three men leaving the cabin, after lunch, it was Polly who told them that they should be back early because she wanted to have some fun tonight.

The men had some plan and took the team and a long two manned saw with them. They told us they were going to drag a large log home and that they were making something. Polly and I wanted to have plenty of time to enjoy our bath, before the men returned, so as soon as they left, we filled the tub and began undressing. Polly offered, that this one time, I should have the first bath, and she helped me into the hot water. She did my back and hair and then began to wash my breasts and down below. Her breasts swayed seductively as she scrubbed and fondled my body so this time it was me who pulled her breast to my lips. I sucked on her nipple as she continued to wash me and when she climbed into the tub with me, I began to kiss her lips.

Polly straddled my body and I could feel her moving her pelvis back and forth as she rubbed her love button against mine. We both wanted this so I rolled her over and became the one on top. I can't say that I had an orgasm, but it was deliciously pleasurable for both of us. There was something else I wanted to do, so I climbed out of the tub and washed her back and hair. When I did her front, she lay back with her head back and her eyes closed. I ran my fingers through the thick hair on her coochie and then worked a finger into her. She felt deliciously tight and slippery. I closed my eyes and thought about what Robert would get to feel tonight while I had her husband's cock inside me.

I wanted to do something else, something I had never done before, so I helped her from the tub and helped her dry herself before leading her into the wagon. The table would have been more comfortable but for what I wanted to do I wanted even more privacy. We cuddled together under the covers and kissed passionately for several minutes. We each had a hand on the other's kitty and we were getting close to our release. Before I could chicken out, I ducked under the covers and snuggled down between her legs. I began to kiss and lick her coochie, tasting a woman for the first time. Polly had a strong orgasm and then pulled me up from below the covers by my hair. She kissed my face, which was covered with her juices, and told me that it was now my turn. I lay back and opened my legs for her but she didn't duck under the covers. Instead, she climbed over me in a sixty-nine position and began to lick my coochie. When I opened my eyes, her kitty was right in front of my face It was swollen and wanting more attention. I began to lick her again and we made each other reach many times over the next hour. Finally, when we were both exhausted, she turned around and began kissing my face. We cuddled till we had the strength to get up and prepare for the men's return.

The men returned around dark and brought with them a huge log. The log was nearly as wide as I am tall and it was seven or eight feet long. They were still very closed mouthed about what they were doing. We had a nice supper but even though the men were tired from cutting wood, they were anxious about the evening activities that, they hoped, were about to unfold. Polly and I were exhausted and sated from when we played earlier in the afternoon. The guys were exhausted too, but they refused our offer to put off playing until tomorrow.

I told William that he would be first in the bath tub tonight and Polly was anxious to help him with his bath. I learned later that William reminded her, very much, of the young man she was interested in, before her parents asked her to marry John. I helped fill the tub with hot water, but then left Polly to wash his back and his hair. Polly and I had talked earlier and had decided that we would not give our men hand relief during their bath because it would only help them last longer when we went to bed. Normally, we would want them to last longer but the numerous climaxes we had shared, during the afternoon, had left us tired and sated. I left Polly to help William and went to join the men at the table I sometimes used for my bed.

The men had opened a bottle of brandy and they poured me a cup too. It burned when it went down, but not as bad as the whiskey I had tasted before, and it had a much better flavor. From the sounds emanating from the curtained off bath area it was obvious that Polly and decided to masturbate William and it sounded like he was enjoying it very much.

I explained to our husbands, that John should take his bath next, while I helped Polly "Tuck William into his bed". Then, he and I could go to the wagon to play while Polly helped Robert with his bath. I tried suggesting, that they could have their fun on the table. I hadn't considered when we would swap back to our own husband. I just assumed that when we no longer heard, the other couple doing it, we would then join them or our partner would return. The men, however, had other plans. John explained that when he had first seen Polly kissing Ray it was, by far, the most exciting thing, he had ever seen. He explained, that after that first time, they never showed any affection, to the other partner, until they had gone to bed in the next cabin. Tonight, he wanted to have those intense feelings again. Robert was no help, as he was anxious to see me with John and he was anxious to be intimate with Polly. I was ok with Robert seeing me as he had seen me with the trapper, but I was kind of nervous about what it would be like to see him making out with my friend Polly. Before I agreed, I made them promise that no matter how exciting tonight was for them, that the next time we would have some privacy.

William came out of the curtained off area, with just a towel wrapped around his waist, and Polly was following him closely holding a small towel over her breasts. The towel hid very little and Robert was the only person there who, as far as I knew, had never seen her boobs. His eyes were glued to her tits as she hurriedly followed William into the cave. As she slipped into the cave, she called out to me, over her shoulder, asking if I was coming. I knew that having two naked women would cause William to cum very quickly so I told her I would be right there.

It only took a few minutes to get the guys lined out to take their own baths. When I entered the cave, Polly and William were making out like teenagers. I slowly stripped off my clothes as I watched them and when William raised up to mount Polly, I slipped in beside them. They clearly wanted each other so as Polly raised and relaxed her legs, I reached between them, grabbed

Williams cock, and guided him into my friend. Her breast was near my face so I sucked a nipple into my mouth and let my hand toy with her bottom while William proceeded to have passionate sex with her.

For the most part, I had always saved my passion for my husband. Okay, maybe not so much with Brad and Jacob, but still those were hurried couplings and I just happened to enjoy them. This was different. They were making love and I knew that I was not needed. When they were changing positions, I slipped out of bed, gathered my clothes and slipped naked out into the cabin area. John was done with his bath, so I sat next to him while Robert was in the tub. The sounds coming from the cave did little to hide the passion that the couple was experiencing. John and I were both totally naked and it just seemed natural. I was afraid that it might hurt Johns feelings to know his wife was making love to William, instead of just having sex with him, so I put my arms around his neck and kissed him to distract his attention. I reached between his legs, and his cock was already hard, so the sound of his wife playing must not have been too painful for him. As I gently stroked him, I remembered how good his added length and girth had felt inside me. Again, I wished I would have some privacy with him tonight.

When Robert was finished his bath, I stood and gave him a passionate kiss. He was naked, like John and I, and the kiss started him on his way to an erection. John came behind me and put his arms around me, hugging me from behind. John asked Robert to sit, on the stool facing us, as he began to fondle my body. It was a little surreal to be letting this man touch me, with the lamp light fully on, and my husband sitting directly in front of me but I found it easy to go with the flow. John began by kissing my neck and rolling my nipple between his fingers. It had the desired effect on my husband and in no time, Robert had a full hard on. My coochie was about eye level with my husband and John wasted no time in reaching around me and plunging his fingers into my very wet slit. John tormented my husband as he explored my body and then had me turn sideways, to my husband, and put my hands on the table. John entered me from behind, and although I had no intention of letting Robert know how good it felt, I heard myself moan loudly as his big cock entered me.

John continued to sex me with my husband watching. He talked to Robert, telling him how tight I felt and that I was the youngest woman he had ever had sex with. He continued on, telling Robert that he was going to shoot his seed inside me. He then asked me if I liked his cock. I looked at my husband, before I answered, and his penis was literally dripping pre-cum. I had no desire to hurt my husband, so I just moaned that it felt good. I thought my husband might cum without touching himself as he watched John having sex with me.

Polly interrupted our fun. She too was naked and carrying her clothes. She had the look of a well sexed woman and blushed as we all looked at her. To take the spotlight off of her, she was quick to ask if we were going to play here, or if we could all go to the wagon and continue. This time I felt myself whimpering as John withdrew his hard shaft from my body. My earlier prediction, that four people on a four-foot wife bed, even if the men would be on top of the women, was correct, it was still very crowded. I pulled John on top of me, hoping to get back to where we were when Polly interrupted us. However, this time John's focus was on watching his wife and my husband.

Robert was like a kid at Christmas, he was touching Polly everywhere, just like he had me on our wedding night. John was hard and I got him inside me, but he was holding very still, apparently to keep from cumming as he watched his wife give herself to my husband. I didn't particularly want to see it, but it was so crowded that they were right in front of my face. They had somehow gotten turned around and my face was inches from where my husband was connected to her vagina.

I did my best to ignore what my husband was doing but it is kind of hard to do when it's happening right next to your face. Even though John held himself very still, I could feel his hard member twitch inside me. Without moving he came inside me. He was still hard, and still not moving, so I rolled us over, as gracefully as that can be done in tight quarters, and rode him. Now, I could move to get my pleasure and John was happy with his face as close as possible to the action. I came and John came a second time but I continued to ride him. Now, I watched the other couple. Polly was clearly thinking about something else. William, I suspect, but Robert didn't seem to notice or mind. His eyes were glued to where John and I were connected while John was probably not even conscious of what I was doing because his eyes were glued to where Robert was entering his wife's love hole.

19Chapter Nineteen

We finished and it was suddenly crowded in the wagon's bunk, so Robert and I slipped out and slept on the table. Robert and I had good reclaiming sex and slept peacefully. The next morning, I was up early and prepared a breakfast of smoked meat, fried potatoes, and biscuits for everyone as they rose for the day. It was surprisingly comfortable and although details were not discussed at the table, John and Polly both said that last night was fantastic. Robert and William also said it was great, albeit for different reasons but they too were satisfied. I just grinned as I considered that I probably still had cum in me from my baby's grandpa and my friend had my husband's cum inside her.

The guys spent the day working on the log they had drug home, they used the saw to shape it and then took hot coals from the stove and used them to hollow out the center just like some of the Indians did when they made canoes. The process went on for three days. When they finished, they had made a wooden bath tub. At first, I wondered why but they began to let me in on their plans. We would be moving on soon. John and Polly would stay in our cabin and continue to offer hot baths and other services to travelers. We had developed a nice little trading post. .Even though, I had only, an average of, one guest each week, I had earned a large amount of money. The guys made money as well by selling grain for the draft animals, food for the travelers, the hardtack I had made, and mostly, drinks of the whiskey Robert had brought from Independence.

One day, when the men had left Polly and me alone at the cabin, we had a gentleman caller. I say gentleman because instead of being filthy and dressed in old clothes and maybe a fur or two, he was neatly dressed. Although, he had been on the trail for several days he was ready for a hot bath. He was also educated and a proper gentleman. Instead of blurting out something crude like, "How much for you to give me that cunt of yours", he arrived and began complementing both Polly and me. He said that he thought I must be Polly's daughter. We visited for nearly an hour before he asked about the baths. We informed him of the fifty-cent cost and he looked us right in the eyes and asked how much for the two of us. He did not seem the least bit embarrassed. I would guess that the man was slightly older than my Father but I knew already that I would have no problem going to bed with him, if he wanted me. Polly, thinking we could make some quick money, told him the four dollars would get the two of us for as long as it took.

The man began laughing for the first time since he arrived. Polly did not know what to think and guessed that she had way over - priced our services. She began to back-peddle but, the man held his hand up to silence her, till he could regain his composure. I busied myself by pouring him a hot cup of coffee and when he was done laughing, he told us that we should not under-value our services. He told us that in mining towns it would cost him twenty-five dollars to spend the night, or as long as it took, with a single woman and that while that number was bit on the high side for the usual traveler, two women should cost at least fifteen-dollars out here. He said that a woman in a brothel or saloon would cost him ten or more dollars and she would expect him to buy her an overpriced drink and then rush him to finish and be gone. He told us that women in dance halls, or hurdy gurdy houses, as they were called, would charge a dollar for a dance and other than maybe getting a bit of a feel, nothing would happen.

Even the women who worked in cribs or a run-down brothel would charge five dollars and they would service twenty-five or more men each night. He made us feel good, as well as a bit embarrassed by our business skills, telling us that we were giving premium service for the lowest rate of a worn out Mexican or Chinese whore. I later learned that some were sold for a dollar or less but then again, I had only charged that much to customers I thought could not afford more. To save face I suggested that I fill the bath tub for him and that when we were done, he would leave, whatever amount he felt was fair for the service I provided. He asked if I wanted part of the money in advance and it was my turn to make him feel good, so I told him that I wanted to have sex with him and if we got paid it would be a bonus. He confirmed that we would both join him and when we agreed, he quickly stripped for his bath. Since he was attractive, and had treated us so well, we really took our time with him. Not only during the bath, but when we went into the wagon, we gave him an amazing amount of attention. We spent nearly three hours pleasuring him in every way we knew, I can't speak for Polly but I made love to him. We finished almost three hours later but had a meal on the table when the men finally returned. The gentleman joined us and left early the next morning, but not before handing me a twenty-dollar gold piece.

With very few exceptions, I enjoyed providing the extras to our guests. I no longer considered it, being a whore, I felt that I was providing, for the men, what they desperately needed and if I happened to enjoy it, then so much the better. What we did with John and Polly was on another level. Polly was my best and only female friend. I liked John, because of how he felt inside me, and because of the connection to Brad. I decided that I did not mind Robert enjoying himself with Polly, in fact, I think I was getting the better deal. It was obvious that Polly and William had something going on, but John didn't seem to care and there had been talk about William staying with John and Polly. Polly was a happy camper, she was getting it from Robert and from William.

Polly and I would talk while the men worked outside and I learned that she was in love with William. She was quick to make it clear that she would never leave her husband because even though they had started with an arraigned marriage, they had developed a love for one another. She had discussed it with John, and he, not only, understood, he actually was pleased that she had found someone who made her happy. He would tell his wife to "Go tuck William in," almost every night, and then make love to his wife when she returned to his bed.

The next day we heard several wagons pull up and hail the house. This was the first time more than one wagon visited at the same time. It turned out to be three wagons with each carrying three men. These men were not the struggling folk who had sold everything for a chance to go to California. These men were from wealthy families, had nice wagons, and best of all, they had plenty of money. They had been on the trail for many weeks and they wanted a hot bath. They were also young and wanted a woman.

Our little cabin was not equipped to handle nine men at once, but we quickly prepared to help them as much as possible. While the men were still outside, we hung several quilts over the entrance to the cave and then, using blankets, created two even smaller rooms. The first held the wash tub and the stove. The second, surrounded the table. We pulled the center divider back and began putting food on the table. Again, since there were so many men, we had them bring in their own plates and fill them from the food we set on the table. They were instructed to go into the cave, to eat and relax. Fortunately, I had a large meal cooking, so I was able to let them get started while we prepared more food. The guests were more interested in what extras we would offer them, than they were in eating or washing themselves. I pulled Robert outside long enough to explain the plan Polly and I had formulated to stay in control of the group of travelers. Robert didn't seem too concerned, but both Polly and I knew, that this could turn into a free-for-all, with the men taking what they wanted and there would be nothing we could do to stop them. I told Robert that he would need to collect all the money and that extras should start at three dollars. I also told him that he should not be afraid to get five dollars for special services, like being first in line or using my mouth and vagina. I admonished him, that he would get more than five dollars, for any special services that were gross, like cumming on my face or in my mouth. I explained our plan to make two small areas next to the bath tub, so the guys would be freshly bathed, because neither Polly nor I wanted to put a sweaty cock into our bodies. Since Polly and I would be very busy, until very late, I put him and William in charge of making breakfast. Robert had a look on his face, like I had slapped him, with the suggestion that he cook, but he wisely kept his mouth shut.

Things began to get rowdy even as the men came to fill their plates. They were not shy about reaching out to grab our bottoms and a few even grabbed our boobs. When I protested, saying I was not a whore, they just laughed and said that they knew we were not whores but they knew soiled doves would not care if they were shown a little attention. I certainly did not like being referred to as a soiled dove, but decided that now was not the time to have that argument.

After everyone was fed, we pulled the center curtain closed and filled the tub with hot water. I am sure Polly knew what to do, but I let her watch me while I gave the first man his bath, to make it last a little longer, I trimmed their finger and toe nails. It was easy to keep them interested by giving their penises a few tugs, ever so often, and by not complaining when they grabbed my now swollen breasts. When I had my man nice and clean, I got him out of the tub and dried him off while Polly began to drain and refill the tub with hot water.

I was looking forward to spending time with this man, he wasn't the one who compared me to a soiled dove, as I led him into the next curtain, where we had put several blankets on the table. Unfortunately, my first man had the same problem my husband had on our wedding night, he was barely inside me when he came. Since he wasn't my husband, and since there were eight other men waiting their turn, I cleaned him up, kissed him, and then sent him back to the cave with a suggestion that, next time, he would last longer. Polly finished washing her man in record time and led him to the second room so I poked my face through the curtain, into the cave, and asked who was next.

Some were good and some were less good but it didn't take all that long to have everyone washed. The fact that there were nine of them, let Polly have my first man as we began the second round, and I had her first man. This time I let Polly use the wagon and I continued to use the table as a bed. I had three loads of sperm in me and one load on me. I tried to tease man number three by keeping my legs together when I raised them. He pushed his cock between my legs and as he rubbed between my wet furrow, he came without ever entering me. I felt a bit bad for him, I didn't care about what I got out of it, because this wasn't about love or even about me reaching a climax. I was going to service as many of these men as possible, to make a lot of money for our group. Between guests, I cleaned myself, as best I could, with a rag to make it better for the next guy.

During the second and third round we each did nine or ten men. This time, they had recently gotten off after we washed them and, they lasted much longer. After three or four I was very sore so when the next guy came in, I used my mouth. I planned to let him shoot his perm into my vagina but he held my head on his cock until he came in my mouth. The sperm wasn't that bad and my kitty appreciated the break. After that I used every trick to get the men ready before they entered me. They were not married and most loved to look at my naked body so rather than staying nude, like Polly was, I quickly dressed between each guest and then undressed for them. This exciting them before I gave them a good suck. By the time I spread my legs for them, they were very excited and ready to cum. Not as fast as some did the first time, and even with being a bit sore, I had a couple good climaxes.

Robert, William and John actually did a pretty good job making breakfast for everyone except for the biscuits were harder than the hardtack I made. Polly and I had our last customer, I guess I just as well call them that, when the sun was beginning to rise. We went to the wagon to sleep. Even though I wanted to play with Polly again, before we left, neither of us was wanting anything but sleep. We woke just before noon and we were both terribly sore down there. We were walking gingerly as we prepared the mid-day meal. After the men were fed, we used the curtains for privacy and douched ourselves with a mixture of water, vinegar, and Iodine. It burned like fire but washed us out and after the burning stopped, we felt better.

I expected my coochie to be sore; I expected my breasts to be tender from all the man handling they had received, but I was totally surprised that my whole body ached like when I had worked really hard, only this was much worse. I had just spent ten hours bucking hard against these men and now I was sore.

The men apparently liked the services we had provided because they decided to stay another day. I wasn't sure if I could do it again but the men had been drinking and playing cards in the cave for most of the day and were ready to start enjoying Polly and me. We decided that tonight we would do things much the same as last night but today I would be in the wagon and Polly would use the table. The man who paid to be first was anxious to be inside me and obviously I wanted to keep that to a minimum. When we were alone in the wagon, I undressed him and then undressed for him. I used the time to see what excited him and he said that he thought any woman who sucked was a whore but the idea of rubbing his cock between a woman's breasts excited him. I had brought a small jar of lard in the wagon and rubbed it between my boobs. When he placed his cock between my boobs, and I pushed them together to create a warm tunnel, he came in just a few strokes. Most of it landed on my face and I normally hate that but today it was a small price to pay to let my kitty have a rest. I wiped my face and spent a few minutes cuddling with him as a reward.

The rest of the day and most of the night was spent about the same. Of course, some of the men wanted to push their cocks into me and would not consider anything else but many enjoyed my hands, my mouth, my boobs, even between my tightly pressed together legs. One guy wanted to have sex with my back door. I refused, but we made a deal that he could stick his finger in there, and pretend, while I sucked him off. His finger felt weird but I made him use a lot of lard and it did not hurt. I had heard that some wives made their husbands use the back door when they had their visitor or when they were at the time when they might get pregnant. His finger was not near the size of his manhood, but I had enjoyed being touched there before, and his finger was not bad either.

We were glad when they left the next morning. They had left a lot of their money with us and had left Polly and I sore. Our guests had depleted a lot of our merchandize; especially our booze. I could not have taken it for another night. I didn't keep count, but as best I could ascertain, I had been sexed 60 times in two days. Not all of them had left their sperm inside me but over forty had cum in me and the rest had cum on me. When Robert and William tallied the receipts, Polly and I had earned over $250 and the men had made over a $100 from selling booze and supplies.   We couldn't believe how much money we had made and even though we were so sore that our husbands could not have us in the conventional way for the next several days, we felt rich.   Even after splitting our share with Polly, I made more money in two days than most wealthy men made all summer.

20 Chapter Twenty

Since Polly wasn't up to sex, William loaded John's wagon with all the furs and most of our cash, to make a quick trip to Independence and replenish our supplies. John and Robert had given him lists of several things they wanted or needed for the summer or for future customers. A quick trip meant five days there, two days to make all of his purchases and then ten days to drive the loaded wagon back to our cabin. William must have pushed the horses pretty hard because he was home in exactly two weeks with everything we needed and he still had some of the money left over.

Of course, there were cases of booze, grain for the animals, staples to keep us cooking in the kitchen and to sell to the travelers. He had also brought a sod cutter because Robert had wanted one, a tent and some lengths of pipe, an auger and a pump. The biggest surprise was that he had bought a used plow that could be pulled with a team of horses and several packages of garden seeds. He also brought a crate filled with chickens so that we had fresh eggs to eat. I never thought William would be willing to work that hard, to raise a garden, but Polly seemed to have changed him. Polly spent most of the night with him, the night of his return, but I had a quick roll with him the next afternoon. Polly and I wanted some time alone so we pushed the men out of the house, telling them to go hunting, while we played. It was as good as it had been the first time and I again, tasted a woman. It dawned on me that a man could lick me there and it would feel good, maybe not as good as a woman because she knew where it felt good, but it would be good. I made a mental note to try it with Robert.

Over the next couple of days, we packed up our stuff and helped John and Polly install their new tub and the stove they had. The days were longer and the old trapper had told Robert about a route that took us to the mountain route of the Santa Fe Trail and then allowed us to follow a small but easy trail straight north to, somewhere in what would eventually become the Colorado Territory, where we would pick up the California trail. The trail north was most likely used by Indians and outlaws, but it was one of very few trails that went North and South. If we somehow missed the California trail, then we would cross the Oregon trail further North. It was kind of fun travelling North with my husband. Even though the trail was not good, we made good progress covering more than 25 miles each day. After about four days the trail became less defined and at times it seemed we were in places that no man had ever been but then we would see signs of previous travelers. We were pretty sure it was Sunday so we used it as a reason to stop and let the horses rest. Robert had plans to use it as a reason to have a lot of sex and I kind of liked that thought, because I had plans for Robert.